If I Come Home

an Our Life in Snowflake Falls Story

Aretta Gordish

Other books in the Our Life in Snowflake Falls series include:

Seasons of Peace - The Christmas Collection
Seasons of Hope - Book One
A Season of Love - Book Two
A Joyous Season - Book Three
A New Season - Book Four
It Happened at the Christmas Bazaar - Book Five
It Happened at the Spring Fling - Book Six
It Happened on the Fourth of July - Book Seven
It Happened at the Harvest Fest - Book Eight
A Christmas Memory - Book Nine
A Valentine's Day to Remember - Book Ten
Until we Meet Again - Book Eleven
A Promise Remembered - Book Twelve
Beneath a Christmas Moon - Book Thirteen
If I Come Home – Book Fourteen

The LORD is near to the brokenhearted and saves the crushed in spirit. Psalm 34:18

Prologue

The bell at St. Timothy Lutheran Church resounded throughout the entire community of Snowflakes Falls joyfully announcing the recent nuptials of Carol Engle and Paul Brunswick. It had been a beautiful wedding with no expense spared, mostly paid for by the groom's wealthy parents who had flown in from Chicago with their noses high in the air.

Paul's parents had wanted the wedding to be held at a posh hotel in Chicago, not at some small church in the middle of Ten-buck-two, as they had called the rural town where Carol had grown up. Despite their annoyance with the location, many in attendance believed it was the loveliest wedding they had ever attended, while others thought is was unnecessarily opulent and a bit too braggadocious for the humble community.

The father of the bride, Magnus Engle, had nervously escorted his first-born child down the aisle. He was a giant of a man at six-foot-five, and yet he cried like a little child when he gave his daughter away. The mother of the bride, Abbigale Engle, or Abby, as she liked to be called, also began to cry the very moment she saw her husband's futile attempt at wiping his tears away. The parents of the groom, Winslow and Cecily Brunswick, had not shed a single tear that day, instead they seemed rather perturbed by the length of the ceremony which had been officiated by Carol's uncle, Rev. Charles Wright.

For Magnus and Abby, the wedding had been bittersweet. They were happy that their daughter had found someone to spend the rest of her life with, but they also knew that Carol and Paul would not be choosing Snowflake Falls as their home, nor would it ever be considered in the future. However, they did love their new son-in-law, believing he had a good head on his shoulders and the wherewithal to take good care of their daughter and future grandchildren.

For Winslow and Cecily, the wedding had simply been bitter...well, mostly for Cecily. Winslow wasn't a big talker, so he rarely revealed his thoughts. It was noted, however, that he had danced with his new daughter-in-law at the reception, and many had noticed the happy smile on his face as he did so. However, Cecily was very vocal about the fact that she had wanted her only child to choose someone who had a better pedigree instead of someone whose only claim to fame was being crowned Miss Corn Queen at the town's annual Harvest Fest. Cecily thought that the small town sweetheart, whom her son, in her opinion had foolishly fallen in love with, was sorely lacking in style and grace. She believed Carol was far from being a classic beauty who would compliment her son's meticulously well-groomed appearance, especially when they were out and about in a social setting.

Despite the fact that Carol's mother-in-law thought that she was just some "local yokel," her family and friends thought that Paul Brunswick must be the luckiest man alive to get someone like Carol Engle to agree to marry him. Carol had been named after her father's grandmother, Carol Bauer, who had been a strong-minded and well-loved member of the community. Her parents had hoped that in giving their daughter the matriarch's name, she might somehow possess even half the strength and tenacity that her great-grandmother had had. As they watched her grow into a beautiful, young woman, they were pleased that she had far surpassed their expectations. Carol was not only strong-minded, she was outgoing and kind. She was confident and had the uncanny ability to say exactly what was on her mind in a clear and concise manner, leaving no one to question what she was thinking. Some people, including her mother-in-law, saw that personality trait as her being headstrong and stubborn, but Carol believed it was necessary for effective communication. Her great-grandmother had believed exactly the same thing.

It was no surprise to anyone when Carol announced that she wanted to become a nurse. She had a loving and compassionate nature about her. However, she was also extremely independent and had an adventurous spirit. That's why she chose to attend a nursing school that was out of state. Though she had loved growing up in the friendly community of Snowflake Falls, she had no desire to remain there. Carol also wanted to travel and see the world, which she did during each of her summer breaks, something her parents weren't very happy about since they rarely saw her. It was the one thing they had always argued about, and it was the one thing Carol wouldn't budge on.

She knew her parents wanted her to remain in Snowflake Falls after she graduated, and though it broke their heart, she made it clear to them that Snowflakes Falls didn't have what she wanted out of life. "You guys have to understand," she would argue, "if I come home, it's just going to be for a short visit. There is a big world outside of this little bubble of a town. As much as you want me to stay, I just can't. I know that I'm never going to find what I'm looking for in Snowflake Falls."

However, she did find exactly what she was looking for in Chicago, including the man of her dreams. During Carol's senior year in college, her wisdom teeth continued to bother her to the point that she knew she was going to have to have them removed. She made an appointment with a dentist, and as soon as she laid eyes on Dr. Paul Brunswick, she was, as her great-grandmother would say, completely twitter-pated. He was ten years older than her, but it was always said that Carol was an old soul, so she never even noticed the age difference. In her opinion, he was perfect in every way. It didn't take long at all for her to announce to her family and friends that she was in love.

Paul fell hard for her, too. After her surgery, he stopped by her dorm room to bring her flowers. Once she was fully recovered, he began to wine and dine her, taking her out every weekend to expensive restaurants, introducing her to a lifestyle she had only dreamed about. He would lavish her with jewelry and weekly floral arrangements. Within just a few months, his attempts to woo her had paid off. Just as soon as Carol graduated from nursing school, she agreed to marry him. Her family had been ecstatic. However, Paul's mother began to worry and subtly tried to persuade him to rethink the engagement. The more she cautioned him, the more he pushed to get married as soon as possible.

After the wedding, they honeymooned in Europe, then went back to Chicago where Carol moved in to his high rise apartment in a swanky, downtown neighborhood of Chicago. She got a job as an ER nurse in a hospital not far from their home, and worked all during their first year of marriage. They easily fell into a nice routine which included Paul taking her out almost every weekend. The other nurses at Carol's work were jealous because he sent her flowers every Friday just to let her know how much he loved her. By all appearances, Paul and Carol were the perfect couple, living the perfect life.

When Carol learned that she was pregnant, she had been extremely happy. However, she was a little disappointed that Paul didn't seem to be as excited as she was. He assured her that he was happy, too, just nervous about being a father. He also knew that the addition of a baby would require them to move out of the one bedroom apartment he had loved, and into a house in the suburbs. He wasn't sure if he was ready for owning a home and all the responsibilities that came with it.

After the baby arrived, things slowly began to change in their marriage. Paul didn't seem to be as enamored with their son, Blake, as Carol was. Carol enjoyed being home full-time with her new son, but she began to notice that Paul was spending more and more time at work. When he did get home, he would read the paper, eat dinner, then head to bed early without hardly saying two words to Carol or their son.

Things between the two didn't improve when their second child was born. Little Lizzie had a sweet disposition and was always so pleasant to be around. However, by that time, Blake was the total opposite. He was all boy and always into some sort of trouble. Carol loved the contrast in their personalities, but Paul was annoyed with how both of his children seemed to crave his attention just as soon as he stepped through the front door. He had recently left the dental clinic where he first began working to start his own private practice, something he had always wanted to do. However, he was now away from home at least 12 hours a day. When he got home, the last thing he wanted to do was spend time with his tired wife and clingy children.

The stress of owning a business, managing a home, and taking care of two busy toddlers was beginning to take a toll on their marriage. Carol wasn't sure what to do to fix it, but having a third child was definitely not the answer. The new baby, Zoe, was often sick and cried a lot. Paul rarely held her and seemed determined to avoid her at all cost. Though he wasn't physically abusive, his words became almost cruel and would cut deep into Carol's heart. He had made it clear that he wasn't happy with her appearance or the way she never had time to keep the home clean and orderly. To make matters worse, Paul would often confide in his parents, more specifically his mother, about his unhappiness. Because of that, Carol would get weekly calls from Cecily who often lectured her on how to be a better wife and mother.

Carol knew she didn't dress nice or fix her hair anymore, but she was exhausted. She hadn't lost all the weight she had gained after Zoe was born, so Yoga pants and a sweatshirt were her go-to clothes almost every day. The house didn't get cleaned as often as it should because whenever the kids were napping, Carol would nap with them. She told herself that her marriage would improve once Zoe was older and had outgrown whatever it was that was always keeping her sick and cranky. Carol fully believed that their love was strong enough to pull them through this difficult time in their life. Things would get better, she was certain of it...that is until that cold, rainy evening in November.

Zoe was sick again and was running a high fever. Carol had practically torn the house apart looking for pain reliever to give her, but she couldn't find any. She called her husband at work several times, but he didn't answer or return her calls. When she finally heard his car drive up into the driveway, she sighed with relief as she ran to meet him at the door, carrying the crying one-year old in her arms. "Oh, thank goodness you're finally home! I've been calling you for hours. Why didn't you pick up?"

"Can you give me just two-seconds before I have to hear about how horrible your day was. I'd like to take a shower and change out of these clothes first," he grumbled as he threw his keys on the small table next to the door. He then loosened his tie as he walked around his wife, ignoring both her and the screaming child.

"Paul! The baby...she's sick. She has a fever, and I don't have anything to give her to help it go down. I need you to…"

"So, what's new, Carol?" He growled. "You're probably out of milk and bread, too! By all means, let me go back out into this storm to get all the things that you are constantly forgetting. It's not like I work all day while you stay home in this palace doing nothing but watching TV, eating who knows what, and gossiping with your friends!"

"You know I don't do that!"

"Do I?" His eyebrows arched as he looked her up and down, disgusted by the spit-up stains on the shoulder of the t-shirt he was pretty certain she had been wearing the day before. He shook his head as he eyed the strands of loose hair falling out of the lop-sided ponytail on the top of her head. He looked around the room first noticing the huge pile of unfolded laundry on the couch. He then moved his gaze toward the sink full of dishes in the kitchen, finally stopping on the dump truck and other toys the kids had left on the stairs. "Yes," he said sarcastically, "I can see that you've been very busy!"

"It's just that Zoe wouldn't let me put her down all day. I finally called the doctor, and he put in a prescription for antibiotics for her at the pharmacy. So..."

"I've got to go wait in line at the pharmacy, too?"

"Sorry, but yes. It's probably just an ear infection. The doctor said…"

"I don't care what the doctor said! All I know is that she is the sickest child I've ever seen! What are you feeding her?"

Carol wanted to defend herself, but she didn't want to get into an argument in front of the children. "I'm sorry. I can go, if you'll just watch…"

"No way!" he interrupted. "I'm not watching a crying baby. I'll go get it!" He huffed loudly.

"Thank you," she said quietly, trying desperately to hold back the flood of tears that would soon wash over her if the baby didn't stop crying soon.

"It's going to be a while. I need to take a shower first," he said angrily as he started up the stairs again.

"Paul, wait! She's been crying for hours. Could you please go now."

"Are you kidding me?" He said angrily.

"No, I'm not. Our daughter is very ill."

He huffed again as he threw his hands in the air. "Why in the world did I agree to all these kids! They're nothing but trouble!"

Just then their other children came around the corner. They had heard their parents arguing and came to investigate. When Carol saw them, she gasped, knowing they had heard their father's comment. She glared at Paul and slowly shook her head at him before rushing toward her children. "Let's go see if we can find something for you two to watch on TV."

"But I want to see Daddy!" Four and a half-year-old, Blake, shouted. "He promised he would play with me when he got home from work."

"I know, but Daddy has to go get Zoe her medicine."

"Can I go with you, Daddy?" Three-year-old, Lizzie asked. She ran toward him with outstretched arms, hoping he would pick her up like he used to do.

"Lizzie!" He yelled. "Go watch TV with your brother! It's raining outside, so no, you can't come with me."

Lizzie stomped her foot down hard on the floor, she then began to wail. Blake was so upset after hearing his father yell, that he too began to cry.

"That's it!" Paul screamed. "I'll go get the medicine, but when I come home, I'm packing my bags. This just isn't working for me anymore!"

Carol could no longer control her tears. They began to stream down the side of her face. She was shocked by how callous and cruel her husband was behaving. Blake's eyes widened, not believing he had heard correctly, and Lizzie ran and hid behind her mother, clinging tightly to her legs. In the midst of it all, the baby had somehow fallen asleep in her mother's arms. The silence was deafening.

"Paul," Carol whispered. She had no other words to say.

Paul ran his fingers through his hair a few times then nodded his head as if agreeing with something he was thinking in his mind. "Yeah, I think it's best that we end this, Carol. I just...I don't love you anymore." With that, he grabbed his keys and went back out into the rain, slamming the door behind him. The force caused one of their wedding pictures to crash to the floor, shattering glass in every direction.

Carol looked down at her children and found them both looking up at her, hoping for some answers that made sense to their young minds. "It'll be okay. Daddy just had a bad day at work. Sometimes grownups say things they don't mean to say."

"Daddy doesn't love us?" Lizzie tearfully asked.

"Oh, no, sweetheart. Daddy loves you all very much."

"But...he doesn't love you," Blake said as he wiped at his eyes.

"Daddy is just tired. He'll feel better in the morning."

Carol gently laid Zoe down in her swing and turned it on, hoping the swaying motion would help her stay asleep. She then walked toward the couch, picked up the remote control, and began searching for a children's program to occupy Blake and Lizzie while she cleaned up the glass. She needed to stay as busy as possible so that she wouldn't dwell on the words that echoed over and over in her mind, *I don't love you anymore.*

After she swept up the shattered glass, she folded the laundry, then started on dinner. Her children were going through a fussy eating stage, but they would always eat spaghetti, so for the third time this week, she put a pot of water on the stove to boil. She looked at the clock and realized an hour had past, and Paul still hadn't returned.

She called his cellphone, but he didn't pick up. She knew her kids were hungry, so she went ahead and fed them. By this time, the baby was awake, but thankfully, she wasn't screaming. However, she did want to be held. Though it was challenging with a baby in her arms, she managed to get a bath for Blake and Lizzie, read them a story, and tuck them into bed without any complaints from them.

When she went back downstairs, Paul still wasn't home. She tried not to panic, but she knew that something must be wrong. Had he really meant what he said? Was he leaving her for good this time? He had made that threat before, but they always seemed to work it out. However, he had never told her that he didn't love her anymore.

They had been married for almost seven years. During that time, they had had their fair share of struggles, but she thought things were finally looking up for them. Paul seemed to be doing well with his dental practice, and they had been talking about maybe taking the children to Disney World for Christmas this year. She knew he had been under a bit more stress than usual at work, but she thought things between them were okay. Not great, but okay.

As she thought about that a little more, she knew she was lying to herself. Things had not been okay between them for a very long time. The two hadn't been out in years, and the weekly flowers had stopped just after Blake had been born. He started forgetting her birthday and anniversaries. On Mother's Day he would lavish his mother with expensive gifts, but seemed to forget about her. She wasn't sure what to do, but if it meant going to a marriage counselor she would do it. She would do whatever she needed to do to save their marriage, and she was determined to start just as soon as he got home. She wasn't going to let him go anywhere until the two of them sat down and had a very long, heart to heart conversation.

After another hour past, Zoe was starting to get fussy again. Just as Carol was reaching for her phone to call Paul, the doorbell rang. "Oh, thank God!" She assumed her husband needed help getting the door open. "I thought you would never get here," she said as she opened the door. She immediately took a step back. "I'm sorry," she said as she looked at the two police officers. "I thought you were my husband."

"Mrs. Brunswick?"

"Yes, that's me."

"I'm Officer Garcia, and this is Officer White."

"Dear God…" she whispered the beginning of a prayer, knowing that something awful had happened.

"Ma'am, may we come in?"

The rest of the conversation became just scrambled words after hearing that her husband was dead. After they left, Carol sat down on the couch and cradled her crying daughter in her arms. Exhaustion, confusion, and fear slowly began to swallow her up. Like Zoe, she too began to cry.

Finally, she picked up the phone and called the two people who had always been there for her. As soon as she told her parents the tragic news about Paul, her father simply said. "We're leaving right now. We'll be there tomorrow evening."

From that moment on, Magnus and Abby tried to help Carol see the wisdom in moving back home where they could help her with the children, but Carol was determined to do it on her on. However, she did hope that she might be able to call upon Paul's parents if she needed some help. The first time she did, she regretted it almost immediately.

Winslow and Cecily were devastated by the loss of their only child. Winslow had made an attempt to console Carol during the funeral, but Cecily had barely spoken two words to her. A few weeks after the funeral, Carol had called her mother-in-law to ask if she would come over and watch the children for a few hours while she ran some errands. Her reply was that she wasn't a babysitter and that her son would still be alive if Carol had been a better mother and had gone out earlier in the day to the get Zoe's medicine herself. Those words had cut like a knife. She never called on Cecily again.

It took a full year for her to finally realize she wasn't going to be able to make it on her own. The only option she had left was to return to the small town where she had grown up. It was, however, the last place she wanted to go, knowing that everyone who thought she had such a perfect life would finally come to learn just how imperfect her life had been.

It had been a difficult phone call for her to make, taking her several attempts at staying on the line long enough for someone to answer. When she heard her father's voice, she choked back her sobs long enough to say, "If I come home..."

"I know," her father had said. "It's just for a visit. We won't pressure you to stay."

"No, Dad. I'm coming home to stay, but I don't want you and Mom to feel like you have to take care of me. I won't be a burden to you or anyone else, and I certainly don't want anyone feeling sorry for me."

"You would never be a burden to us. We love you so much, sweetheart."

"I know that you do, but you always want to try and fix all my problems, and this is one I have to fix on my own. I'm going to have to go back to work. I eventually want to find my own place. I need..."

"Carol..." She could hear her father's deep sigh. "Just come home."

Two weeks later, she was on the road to Snowflake Falls.

Chapter One

"You're going to burn a hole in that window?" Magnus teased his wife. "Stop worrying. She'll be here soon."

"Why is it snowing out there? There's already five or six inches on the ground!"

Magnus laughed at that. "Have you forgotten where you live. It's the first of December in Snowflake Falls. I'm surprised we don't already have a foot of snow on the ground."

"I know, but why couldn't it wait until Carol got here with the kids? I'm worried about her."

"Dear, she grew up in this town. I taught her how to drive in the snow. She'll be just fine."

"I know, but Zoe is probably giving her fits."

"Zoe is probably sleeping. Most kids do that in the car."

Abby sighed as she moved away from the window. "They'll be okay, won't they?"

"As far as driving here?"

"No, I mean...just okay with everything."

"Carol has always been very strong. She still has her nursing license. She'll easily get a job at the hospital or clinic. We'll help her find a nice place to live, but until then, she and the kids can stay here as long as they need to."

"I know this wasn't what you planned for your retirement, but..." Abby sighed.

"Carol and the kids need us right now. We can always travel next year."

"I can't believe Paul didn't have life insurance! I mean, who doesn't have life insurance?"

"He was young. I'm sure he didn't think it would be needed. Besides, starting his own practice was probably so consuming that he didn't have time to think about anything else."

"Obviously! He couldn't even think about paying his mortgage. He was behind two months and his business was deep in debt. How could Carol not have known that? Things must have been just awful for her."

"I think he just got in over his head. Carol was probably too busy with the kids to notice. You know Paul, though. I'm sure he had some long term goals...he just...well he didn't live to see those come to fruition."

Abby sighed again as she shook her head. "I'm just so angry he left her with all that debt. His parents have tons of money. You would think they would have offered to help. You saw how much they paid for the wedding. They wouldn't even let us pay a dime."

"I know. I don't understand it myself, but Abby..." He shook his head, not wanting to have this conversation again. "I know I don't have to tell you this, but Paul is gone. Winslow and Cecily lost their only child. I can't imagine the pain they have suffered. There's no reason to be angry. Carol is going to be just fine. Her house sold, and the business was taken over by one of Paul's associates. She may not have anything left, but she's no longer in debt. Also, the children are receiving survivor benefits. They'll be okay. She's made the right decision to come stay with us. I'm sure she'll be back on her feet in no time."

"I hope so." Abby wrapped her arms around her husband's waist, needing to feel his strength. "It's going to be nice having the children here, especially for Christmas. We hardly ever got to see them."

"I can't remember the last time she was home. I guess it was for Philip's wedding."

"I believe so. She only stayed a few days, though. The kids have never been here in the winter. I don't know what they're going to think about all this snow."

"They're kids. They're going to love it!" Magnus said. "I've already got three sleds waiting for them in the garage."

"Before you go taking them out in the snow, let's make sure they have proper coats and gloves."

"Already taken care of," Magnus said with a grin on his face.

"You really are excited they're coming, aren't you?"

"Yeah, I really am." He smiled. "Now that I'm retired, I have all the time in the world just to be a grandfather."

"You are the best grandfather a kid could ever have. Josie's kids have been spoiled rotten by you."

"Hey, you've taken part in a lot of that spoiling yourself."

"Guilty as charged!" She laughed. "It's going to be so wonderful having all my children and grandchildren close by. I was thinking we should invite all the family over this weekend. You know, just to welcome Carol back home again."

"Let's make sure she's up to it. Philip and Josie will be here soon, that may be all the welcome she can handle for the time being."

"Yeah, maybe you're right. She doesn't sound like herself when I talk to her on the phone. She's sounds so down."

"It's going to take some time, but I know Carol. She'll come out of this just fine."

Abby walked back to the window. When she saw headlights pulling into the driveway, she ran to the coat closet. "They're here!" She pulled out her coat and flung it around her shoulders. "Come on, Papa! Let's help get the kids out of the car."

She excitedly opened the front door and stepped out onto the porch. However, her smile quickly turned to a frown as she watched her youngest daughter, Josie, get out of her car."Oh, it's just Josh and Josie," Abby said disappointingly.

"Just Josh and Josie?" Josie said after hearing her mother's disappointment at their arrival. "Gee, thanks Mom! It's good to see you, too." She laughed.

"Sorry, sweetheart. I thought you were Carol."

"She's not hear yet?" Josie unbuckled her one-year-old son, Noah, then pulled him out of his car seat while her husband, Josh, helped their five-year old, son, Adam unbuckle his seat belt.

"Nana!" Adam yelled as he ran all the way up to the porch and wrapped his arms around his grandmother's legs.

"Hi, buddy! Are you excited about seeing your cousins?"

"Yes, but Noah's not! He's giving Mama trouble."

"Yes, he is!" Josie said as she walked up the steps, handing Noah to her father. "Here ya go, Papa, he's all yours!"

"Are you being a grumpy pants?" Magnus squeezed his grandson, then placed a kiss on the top of his head.

Noah wrapped his arms around Magnus' neck and giggled with glee.

"Oh, sure now he's happy," Josie said as she rolled her eyes. "He's teething, so watch the drool." She placed a cloth on her father's shoulders.

"I don't mind a little drool. Let's get out of this cold, though. I'm not a fan of frozen drool." He chuckled.

Just as soon as they shut the door, a horn honked outside. "That must be her!" Abby opened the door again and looked outside. "No, it's just Philip and Tammy." She sighed heavily. "Oh, I hope everything's all right with Carol and kids."

"She probably just stopped to get something to eat," Josie said.

"I know, it's just this weather is so awful."

"The roads are okay. We didn't have a problem getting here," Josh said, trying to encourage his mother-in-law.

"Hi, everyone! Is Carol here yet?" Philip asked as he helped his very pregnant wife up the steps and into the house.

"No," Abby said. "She called when she got to Pinecrest a couple of hours ago. She should be here by now, though. You didn't happen to pass her along the way, did you?"

"I don't know. What's she driving these days?"

"A blue minivan."

Philip turned around and looked down the street and saw headlights heading in their direction. "Oh, you mean like the one coming up the street right now?"

Abby stepped around him and looked down the street. She then breathed a huge sigh of relief. "Yes! She's here everyone!" She walked down the steps and then out to the sidewalk.

There wasn't any room left in the driveway, so Carol had to park next to the curb. As soon as she came to a stop, Abby opened the sliding door of the van and found all three of her grandchildren sleeping. "Oh, they are just so precious!"

"They just went to sleep," Carol whispered before getting out of the van. She walked around to the other side where her mother was standing. "Sorry, I'm late. After we stopped to eat, I let the kids stretch their legs for a bit."

Abby reached for her daughter and wrapped her arms around her, squeezing her tight. "I'm so glad you're here, Carol."

"It's good to see you, Mom." She then looked up and saw her father and the rest of her family walking toward her. "Hi, everyone!" She waved her hand, then stepped toward her father. When he wrapped his strong arms around her, she felt her body relax for the first time in almost a year. She finally felt safe. She looked up and almost cried when she saw his misty eyes. "Hi, Daddy."

"Hi, sweetheart." When he saw how thin and tired she looked, he didn't trust himself to say anything else. He hated that his daughter was suffering and would have taken it all upon himself if he could have.

Carol then hugged her brother and then her sister-in-law. "Tammy, you look so good!"

"One more month to go!"

"Maybe you'll have a New Year's baby?"

"That's what Philip is hoping for, but at this point, I don't care when she decides to come." Tammy laughed as she rubbed her large belly.

"I'm really happy for you guys. I can't wait to meet my first niece. Do you have a name picked out, yet?"

"We're thinking, Sonja, after grandma," Philip said.

"She would have loved that," Carol said. She then turned to Josh and Josie, hugging Josh first then her sister, giving her an extra long squeeze. "I've missed you so much, Josie."

"I've missed you, too. It's going to be so nice having you home again."

"Well," she said as she turned her head back toward the van. "I'm going to need some help getting the kids out. Lizzie won't wake up, so she'll just need to go straight to bed. Blake will be mad at me if I don't wake him up. He's wanting to play with Adam. If we can keep Zoe asleep, that will be a godsend. She didn't sleep well in the hotel last night, so she's exhausted."

Abby reached inside the van and began to gently shake Blake. "Blake, you're here. Adam is so excited to see you."

"Adam?" Blake's eyes flew open. He then jumped out of the van. "Where is he?"

"He's inside the house waiting for you," Abby said. "But how about a hug for your Nana first." Blake gave his grandmother a quick hug before running into the house screaming Adam's name the entire way.

"That was easy enough." Abby laughed. She then reached for Lizzie. She was careful not to shake her too much as she scooped her up out of her seat and into her arms. "I'll take her upstairs. She'll be in Josie's old room."

"Just put her in the room I'll be in. She's been having nightmares lately, so I've been letting her sleep with me."

"That sounds like a good idea," Abby said as she carried the sleeping child inside the house.

Carol reached for Zoe and almost had her out of her car seat when she woke up and began to cry. "It's okay, Zo-zo. We're at Papa and Nana's house." She pushed the child's golden locks out of her eyes then lifted her out of the seat.

"Philip, Josh, and I will bring in your bags. You all take the kids inside where it's warm," Magnus said.

Once everyone was settled inside, Abby went into the kitchen to make some hot chocolate. Lizzie was sound asleep just as her mother had said she would be. Blake and Adam were playing cars in the corner while Zoe was content to sit on her Papa's lap near the fire. No one was really talking, they were just enjoying having the entire family together again. It had been a very long time since this had happened.

"Who want's hot cocoa?" Abby said as she entered the room carrying a tray of mugs.

"Thanks, Mom. That sounds good. I forgot how cold it can get here," Carol said. She tucked her feet up underneath herself then reached for one of the mugs. "Hey, how come you all don't have a tree yet? You usually have it up on Thanksgiving."

"We thought it would be fun to wait for the kids to help pick one out," Magnus said.

"They'll love that. We didn't have a tree last year with everything...well, you know."

"We know," Abby said. "That's why we wanted to wait for you all to get here."

As Carol blew the steamy drink to help cool it off, her eyes moved slowly around the room, observing each of her family members. Josh and Josie were sitting together on the love seat. Josh was holding Noah on his lap with one arm and had the other one wrapped around Josie's shoulders. Josie was snuggled up close to her husband, letting her head rest on his shoulder. Every now and then, Josh would lean down and kiss the top of his son's head, then do the same to his wife.

Over on the couch, Tammy had laid her head on Philip's lap, and he was gently running his fingers through her hair. Her eyes were closed, so Carol assumed his gentle touch had caused her to go to sleep. At one point, Philip noticed the baby kick and placed his hand over the spot where he had just seen a little foot. Tammy opened her eyes and smiled as she covered his hand with hers.

Carol was glad that her brother and sister had found such happiness and love. It had been a very long time since she and Paul had shared the kind of affection she was witnessing in the room. She tried not to think about Paul's last words to her, but watching how much in love her siblings were, she knew that it was true that Paul had stopped loving her...or maybe he had never really loved her at all.

She took a deep breath in and looked over at her father. He was swaying back and forth, causing Zoe to struggle to keep her eyes open. Her mother walked over to her father and placed her hand on his shoulder, giving it a gentle squeeze. He looked up at her and winked. Carol had grown up seeing her father wink at her mother like that. It was his secret way of silently telling her how much he loved her.

When Abby leaned down and kissed Magnus on the cheek, Carol couldn't control her emotions any longer. She placed her mug on the coffee table then lowered her head and began to sob.

Abby rushed to her daughter's side and wrapped her arms around her. "Oh, honey! What's wrong?"

"I'm sorry, it's nothing. I'm just...really tired. Do you all mind if I just go to bed."

"No, not at all. Don't worry about Blake, we'll get him settled in."

"Thanks. I'll take Zoe up with me." She sniffed as she wiped at her eyes, embarrassed that she hadn't been able to control her emotions. "She'll probably sleep better if she's with me and Lizzie."

Josie stood up and took Zoe from her father. "I'll carry her up, Dad."

"Thanks, Josie," Carol said as she followed her sister up the stairs.

Josie stayed to help Carol get Zoe into bed next to Lizzie. When Carol turned to say goodnight to her sister, Josie took her hand and pulled her out into the hallway. She then wrapped her arms around her and whispered near her ear. "Okay, what's going on?"

"Nothing, really. Like I said, I'm just tired."

"Carol...this is me you're talking to you. I know that's not why you were crying downstairs."

"You were always good at reading people."

"Yes, I am, so what's going on?"

"It's just seeing all the love downstairs…I know that I'll never have that."

"But you did have that, and those memories will always be with you."

"Josie…" Carol shook her head. She desperately wanted to talk to someone about what had been going on with her and Paul, but she was too embarrassed to say anything. Everyone thought she had had the most perfect life. How could she tell them that it had all been a lie.

"I know you miss him." Josie pulled Carol close and squeezed her gently. "It will take some time, but everything will be okay. I've been praying for you every day. I know that God has a plan for you."

"I just hope He lets me in on it sometime soon. Right now, I have no idea what to do."

"Well, to begin with, you just breathe. We're all here for you, Carol. We're going to help you with anything you need. You know that, right?"

"Yeah, I know." She just wasn't sure what it was that she needed.

Chapter Two

It had a been a busy and very emotional first few days for Carol. Everyone assumed her tears were due to the fact that she was still mourning the loss of her husband. However, the shock of Paul's death had worn off a long time ago. It had been replaced with anger in knowing that there was so much that he hadn't told her.

His dental practice hadn't been doing well at all. On the day he had died, his hygienist had quit because she hadn't been paid for several months. Also, on that same day, he had stopped by the bank and closed out their savings account, using every dime to pay off other debts he was behind in paying. A few weeks after his death, she realized there was absolutely no money at all for her to live on. She had to apply for help with the state just so her kids would have food to eat.

She would never forget the first time she was in a grocery store and pulled out the card the state gave her to use for groceries. She was having trouble figuring out how to use it. The cashier was new and didn't know either, so she got on the loud speaker and called for a manager to come help with a "food stamp" card. Carol's cheeks turned bright red as she looked at the line forming behind her. She noticed one of the mother's from Blake's preschool whispering to another woman. The two began to laugh as they stared in her direction. She wanted to just leave the groceries and get as far away from there as possible, but her kids had already gone two days without milk.

Her parents had helped quite a bit, especially after she had swallowed her pride and admitted to them that she was broke and was faced with an incredible amount of debt that she had no idea how she would be able to pay. They never judged her or asked any questions, but she could tell they didn't understand what had happened. The problem was that Carol didn't understand, either. Paul had kept it all hidden from her.

Being a single mother of three young children often left her in a panicked state. She knew that her staying home with the children was no longer an option. She would need to get a job. Thankfully, she already had an interview at the clinic this morning and her mother and father were more than happy to watch the children while she was working.

Over the past few days, she had managed to enroll Blake in school, and Lizzie was starting her first day of preschool at St. Timothy Lutheran Church. Josie had already stopped by to take Blake to school, giving Carol some extra time to get herself and Lizzie ready. Carol's cousin, Harriet Carrington, was the teacher at St. Timothy Preschool and had already formed a special bond with Lizzie over the weekend. This morning, Lizzie was beside herself with excitement as her mother tried to comb her hair.

"Sit still, Lizzie, or your hair will be a mess."

"I can't help it. I'm so excited! Harriet said that I was going to make lots of new friends."

"You will, but be sure to call her Mrs. Carrington when you're at school."

"Why?"

"Because she's your teacher, so you need to address her as your teacher instead of as your cousin."

"But she is my cousin."

"I know, but while you're at school, she's your teacher. I know it's hard to understand, but it's just the way it has to be. Okay?"

"Okay, I'll try to remember."

Carol gathered all of Lizzie's curly blond hair into a ponytail then secured it all together with a pink rubber band. "All done! You're now officially ready for your first day of school."

Carol looked at herself in the mirror and frowned. The skirt and suit jacket she wore were a bit outdated, but at least she fit into them again. It was no longer snug like it had been when she had worn it to Paul's funeral. Her hair was longer than it had ever been and badly in need of a fresh cut, but that was a luxury she could no longer afford. So instead, she had attempted to curl it. Lizzie had said she looked very pretty even though Carol believed she could have spent a little more time on it. She gave up when she kept burning her fingers on the curling iron.

"What do you think? Should Mommy put a little makeup on for my interview this morning?"

"Yes! Can I have some, too!"

"Sure, just a little." She brushed a little blush on her daughter's cheeks even though they were already red from being outside every day with her Papa playing in the snow. "There you go. You look like a little princess!"

Lizzie jumped down off the counter, then ran to her room to get her coat and the new backpack her grandmother had bought for her. She came back with her coat on, but she was struggling with the backpack.

"Here, let me help you." Carol reached for the straps of the backpack and pulled them over Lizzie's shoulders. She then zipped up her coat. "Go say goodbye to Papa and Nana before we leave."

Magnus and Abby hugged Lizzie then stood by the door and watched her skip out to the car. "Have fun!" Magnus called out. "We'll have cookies and milk when you come home!" Abby yelled, waving goodbye.

Once they were on the road, Carol was careful to drive slow since the roads were icy this morning. Ever since Paul's accident, she found herself being overly cautious when she was driving, especially when the children were in the car. She knew she drove like an old woman, but she didn't care. Safety was more important to her than anything else.

When she reached the church, she came to a complete stop before turning into the parking lot. Just as she started to turn, she heard the screeching tires of the car behind her as it came to an abrupt stop just inches from hitting the rear end of her van. The driver pressed hard on the horn before speeding around her. He then turned into the church parking lot, taking what should have been her place in the drop off line.

Carol's heart was pounding from the near miss. "My goodness!" She said under her breath. "The people around here drive worse than they do in Chicago."

She drove up behind the small, sporty car and watched as a man jumped out, then hurriedly ran around the car to open the passenger door. He reached inside the car and pulled out a little boy who was crying and kicking his feet. He placed him on the sidewalk, then took his hand and tried to pull him to the front door, but the little boy dug his feet into the ground refusing to go.

"Oh brother!" Carol said as she shook her head. "At this rate, we'll be here all day. Come, on Lizzie, we'll just get out here so that you're not late for school."

She got out of the van, then slid open the side door to let Lizzie out. She then took her daughter's hand and walked over to where the man was still struggling with the child. "You know, if you wiped that frown off your face and smiled at the child, you might be able to coax him into going inside."

"Excuse me?" The man looked up, surprised to find someone standing there. He stared at her for several moments before finally saying, "And just who might you be?"

"Oh, I'm just the woman driving that blue van over there...you know the one you almost plowed into just before you dangerously sped into the parking lot in front of me."

"I didn't almost run into you, but if I had, it would have been your fault."

"My fault?" Carol's mouth dropped open as she brought a hand up to her chest. "You're joking, right?"

"No, I'm not. First, you were driving way too slow, then you just stopped in the middle of the road."

"I was turning into the parking lot."

"You could have turned without completely stopping like that, and you could have also given me a warning by turning your blinker on! You were being a hazard."

"No, I was being safe. The roads are icy, and...I'm sure my blinker was on!" Though, the more she thought about it, she wasn't sure if she had put her blinker on or not. It was a bad habit she had. It had always driven Paul crazy.

"There was no blinker," he said angrily, then added, "Look, I don't have time to argue with you. I'm already late and as you can see, my son has decided to throw a royal fit!" He looked down at his son and pointed his finger at him. "Knock it off, Kyle. I don't have time for this!"

"You never have time for anything!" The little boy screamed, then ran inside the building, leaving his father behind.

"I suppose I better go make sure he makes it to his classroom."

"Yeah, I suppose you better." Carol said sarcastically. However, she did feel a little sorry for the man. She had had her fair share of early morning fits when Blake was in preschool. Paul had refused to take him to school, so if nothing else, she had to hand it to the man for at least trying...even if he was rude and drove like a lunatic.

"Who was that man, Mommy?" Lizzie asked as they made their way to the preschool classroom.

"I don't know, sweetheart, but I bet his little boy could use a friend today. I think he's having a bad day. Do you think you could be his friend?"

"Yep! Bye, Mommy!" Lizzie pulled her hand away and walked as fast as she could the remainder of the way to the classroom. Just as she was about to enter the room, she ran right into the little boy's father who was rushing out the door. She cried out as she fell to the floor, landing on her bottom.

"Hey!" Carol yelled as she hurried toward them.

Without saying a word, the man reached down and grabbed Lizzie's hands, hoisting her back up onto her feet. He then patted her on the top of her head a few times before turning to leave again.

It was obvious to Carol that he was in a hurry, but he had just knocked her daughter over which infuriated her. He tried to step around her, but she moved at the same time, blocking his way. "You owe my daughter an apology."

"She's fine…now if you would excuse me, I'm in a hurry. Please, step aside."

"No." She crossed her arms across her body and widened her stance.

"No?" He was astounded by her reply.

"That's right. Not until you tell my daughter that you're sorry for knocking her to the floor like that."

For just a brief moment the two stared deep into each other's eyes. She noticed that his hair was the exact same color as his soft brown eyes. He noticed right away that her eyes were green with golden specs. As his eyes roamed across her face, he thought she was pretty and wondered why he had never seen her before. She thought he was in need of a shave, and then again thought maybe not. The short growth of hair on his face gave him a rugged, masculine look she found appealing.

"Look, I don't have time to go back inside the classroom to apologize to your daughter. Now, I'm asking you for the last time to please move out of my way."

She stubbornly shook her head. She didn't care how nice looking he was, she wasn't going to move until he apologized.

"Okay, fine!" He's nostrils flared as he inhaled deeply.

At first Carol thought she had won the battle. However, her victory was short-lived when in one swift move he reached out his hands, grabbed her around the waist, then lifted her off the floor.

"Put me down!" Carol yelled as she tightly grasped his shoulders.

"I intend to, but over here…out of my way!" He said as he placed her back down. He then hurried out the door before she could say another word.

Carol was so outraged she could hardly breathe. She felt tears of anger sting her eyes as she quickly breathed in and out to try to calm herself down. It took a while, but when she finally composed herself, she peeked her head inside the classroom to check on Lizzie. She was sitting at a table next to the little boy who had thrown a fit. They were both giggling. Carol waved to her cousin, Harriet, then turned to leave knowing her daughter was going to be just fine.

However, she was pretty certain that she wasn't going to be fine until she found out who that guy was and give him a piece of her mind!

Chapter Three

"Mrs. Brunswick, please come in and have a seat," Amanda Price, the clinic administrator, greeted Carol.

"Thank you," Carol said nervously as she combed her fingers through her hair to tidy up as much as possible. "The wind has really picked up out there."

"Oh, I know. Another storm is blowing in. I understand that you are from here, though, so our crazy winters won't be too shocking for you."

"Chicago, where I was living, can be just as cold, so no, I don't mind it at all."

"That's good. One less thing to worry about. You'd be surprised how hard it can be to find good help around here simply due to the weather."

"I can imagine, but you'll be happy to know that I actually like the cold weather."

"Well, we have plenty of that, so you should be very happy." She then turned to the woman sitting next to her. "Let me introduce you to Sarah Keller. It's her position that we're interviewing for. As you can see, she's expecting and has decided to stay home with her baby."

Carol looked over and smiled at the swollen woman who looked as if she was due any day now. "Congratulations! Is this your first?" Carol asked.

"Yes, and I'm just miserable. I've already past my due date."

"That's right, so as you can imagine, we are desperate to fill her position as soon as possible. Sarah has been gracious to stay as long as she possibly can, but something tells me that won't be much longer." Amanda turned her head toward Sarah and grinned.

"I'm very familiar with several of your family members, Carol," Sarah said. "You may not remember, but your sister,

Josie, and I were in school together. I attended several parties and sleepovers at your house."

"Sarah Weiner?" Carol looked at her closely, finally recognizing the woman.

"That's me." Sarah nodded her head and grinned. "Keller is my married name."

"Oh, my gosh! It's good to see you again. It's been a while." The last time Carol had seen Sarah she had bad skin and braces on her teeth. She was amazed by her grownup transformation. "You've really changed since the last time I saw you."

Sarah laughed as she rubbed her hands across her rounded belly. "Yeah, I've put on a little weight."

"You look wonderful. It really is good to see you again."

"It's good to see you, too. I never imagined I would see you back in Snowflake Falls, though. You always wanted to get out of this town."

"Well, things have a way of...changing." She tried to offer a smile, but instead she was only able to sigh.

Sarah's eyes filled with compassion. "I'm so sorry to hear about your husband. That must have been very difficult."

"Yes, it was. So..." She ran her damp hands across her lap, suddenly feeling nervous. She wanted to ask when the actual interview would start, but she knew it would be unprofessional for her to do so.

"We're just waiting for Dr. Bradley," Amanda said, sensing Carol's impatience. "You would be working for him. He's here, but he needed to meet with a patient first. We'll go ahead and get started, though. Since Dr. Bradley is our pediatrician, I guess my first question would be to ask if you've had experience working with children?"

"I was mostly an ER nurse, so I have worked with pretty much every age group."

"Oh, I see." Amanda looked down at the file in front of her, tapping her pen against the table top. "Have you ever given immunizations? I can't imagine you would have done much of that in the ER."

"I am very competent at giving injections. I was also known as the IV queen," Carol said with a smile. "I always got the needle in on the first try."

"Well, I doubt you would be giving IVs here in the clinic. Have you ever had to give an IV during an office visit, Sarah?"

"Not that I recall." She shook her head. "Lots of injections, though...and lots of crying children to try to soothe afterwards."

"Yes, I would think patience would be an attribute one must possess for this position," Amanda said. "I'm sure in the ER you were used to working in a fast-paced environment, is that correct?"

"Oh, absolutely. It was always hectic, but I can handle the fast pace."

"Well, here at the clinic we strive to spend as much quality time as we can with each patient. We don't want our parents or their children feeling rushed."

"Ms. Price, I am a well qualified RN and have excellent training for any nursing position regardless of the work load."

Amanda nodded her head in agreement. "You did go to one of the top nursing schools. I see that you have a B.S. in Nursing, but you only worked as a nurse for a little over a year. I don't see..." She looked over Carol's resume for a moment. "No, I don't see that you worked anywhere else."

"Like Sarah, I chose to stay home with my children. I have three. The youngest is now two."

"So...why are you interested in this position?" She looked up from the file, resting her eyes on Carol's.

Before Carol could answer, the door opened behind her, and a male voice began making his apologies. "I'm sorry I'm late. I hope I didn't miss much."

"Come in, Dr. Bradley. We were just getting better acquainted with Mrs. Brunswick. I was just asking her why she was interested in this position."

Carol took the short break as an opportunity to catch her breath and decide how she wanted to answer the question. Dr. Bradley made his way around the table, pulling out the chair next to Amanda. He then lifted his head to get a better look at the person being interviewed at the exact same moment when Carol looked up at him for the first time. Both of their eyes widened in surprise, but only Carol actually gasped.

"You!" Carol said angrily.

"Uh…" He couldn't think of a single word to say.

However, Carol had plenty to say. "On second thought," she said as she stood to her feet. "This probably isn't the job for me. Thank you for your time, though."

Yes, she needed the job, but there was no way she would ever work with the man who had nearly crashed into her car, knocked her child over, refused to apologize, then physically moved her out of his way.

She didn't care what any of them thought of her as she abruptly left the room.

Chapter Four

"We thought we'd go get the Christmas tree this evening," Magnus said as soon as Carol returned home.

Carol was still upset, but tried to force a smile. "Sure, Dad. The kids will like that."

"Oh, and we've been invited to a Christmas party at Floyd and Nova Emerson's house this weekend. They were sure to include you in the invitation."

"I don't recognize that name."

"That's right, you weren't here for your grandfather's funeral. Floyd and Nova moved here a couple of years ago. They were at the funeral. Floyd was a pastor in Alabama, but he and his wife are retired now."

"Why in the world would they move here?"

"It's a long story. You remember that your grandfather Otis was in prison when he was younger."

"Yes, I remember that story."

"Well, Floyd met your grandfather in prison. I guess they became good friends."

"Yes, but that doesn't explain why this Floyd person is living here now."

"Well, you see, Otis left Floyd his shop in his will."

"Why would he do that?"

"Like I said, it's a very long story, but I'm sure Floyd will be happy to tell you all about it. You're going to just love him. He's loud, boisterous, almost my height, and gives these incredible bear hugs like nothing you've ever felt! His son, Micah, was an NFL football player that used to go by the name "The Monster." He's now our mayor...remember I told you about him on the phone."

"Oh, yeah, I remember you telling me that. They sound like a very interesting family."

"They are. They have really been a nice addition to our small community. Nova took your grandfather's shop and turned it into a tea shop. I know how you like tea, so you might want to go check it out."

"I'll be sure to stop by...but as for the party, I don't think I'm up to that, but be sure to thank them for inviting me."

She started to go upstairs, but Magnus stopped her. "Stop right there, young lady!"

Carol sighed heavily as she turned back around to face her father. He always could see right through her.

"Come sit down and tell me what's wrong."

"Nothing is wrong. I was just going to go check on Zoe," she said looking over the top of her father's head not wanting to look him in the eye.

"Carol...I know that look. You're upset about something."

"I'm just tired."

"Is that why you didn't go to church yesterday?"

"No, I thought Mom told you. Zoe really isn't feeling well."

"She seemed fine today."

"Dad…" She sighed. "I'm just not ready."

"Not ready? What do you mean?"

"To face people."

"That's not why you go to church, Carol."

"I know Dad!"

Her raised voice caused Magnus to arch his brows and ask, "Carol, are you blaming God for Paul's death?"

"No, I would never do that." She shook her head. When she could still see the concern on her father's face, she added. "I do plan to return to church, I just need…"

"Plan to return? Were you not attending church in Chicago?"

"Paul didn't grow up going to church."

"Yes, but you did. You were taught…"

"Dad, please don't lecture me. I know what a failure I've been. I don't need you to remind me!" She started to walk away, but he stopped her yet again.

"Carol, stop! Why would you say you're a failure? You haven't failed any one, sweetheart."

"I don't want to talk about this Dad."

"Okay, but maybe you should go talk to Rev. Pickler. He was a widower, too, maybe he would be able to offer some advice."

"I look forward to meeting Rev. Pickler, but I don't see any reason to talk to him about my personal life as you're suggesting. Yes, my husband died, but I don't see the point in hashing it up over and over again, and I certainly don't need to have a pity party with someone who's been there and done that."

"I don't expect you to have a pity party or even talk about Paul if you don't want to. I do think, however, that it's time for you to really come home. Talking with Rev. Pickler might help in that regard."

"I am home." She whispered as tears sprang to her eyes.

Magnus' face was solemn as he stared at her. He saw her glassy eyes and realized that his daughter was hurting terribly. "I mean you need to return to Christ, Carol. He loves you more than I ever could. He can help you with everything you're going through."

"I'll be at church next week, Dad. I promise."

"I'm not talking about just sitting in a pew. I want you to realize that God is always there for you, and He is always ready to forgive. He can also help fix any problem you're facing. "

"There is nothing for Him to fix." She sighed, weary of this conversation.

"There is a lot for Him to fix, but let's just start with this morning. Something happened that put you in a fowl mood. How bad was it?"

Carol released another heavy sigh then answered, "If you must know, yes, it was bad…really bad!"

He patted the spot on the couch next to him and waited for her to sit down.

"Dad, I really should go check on Zoe," she said as she hesitantly sat down next to him.

"Your mother is giving Zoe a bath. She got a little messy at breakfast." He chuckled. "Now, I want to hear about what happened. Maybe I can help make it better for you."

"I thought I made it clear that I don't need you to fix my problems. I can handle this all by myself."

"Handle what?"

"Fine, I'll tell you, but please don't make a big deal about it, okay?"

"If someone hurt you…"

"I wasn't hurt. It's just…well, there was this guy…and… he totally humiliated me!"

"Who did?"

"Dr. Bradley!"

"Keith Bradley? You had trouble with him this morning?"

"Yes, I did!" She then told him what happened. After doing so, she looked over at her father and frowned because he was grinning. "This isn't funny! Did you hear me tell you that he physically lifted me off the floor."

"Yes, I heard that part." His grin got even wider.

"Dad! I was completely humiliated, and besides that he knocked Lizzie over."

"On purpose?"

"No, but he could have at least said he was sorry."

"Was Lizzie crying?"

"No, but…"

"So, she was fine?"

"Yes, but…"

"Sounds to me like he was just in a hurry."

"I know he was, he was late for an interview at the clinic. Take one guess who was being interviewed!"

Magnus roared with laughter. "This story just keeps getting better and better!"

"There is nothing good about this story! I needed that job. I guess I'll apply at the hospital. I was just hoping to have weekends off. I guess that means I won't be in church after all."

"I'm sure if you just call the clinic back and explain…"

"Explain why I walked out of an interview?" She shook her head. "There's no way they will hire me now, and it's all because of that…that…rude man!"

"He's a nice man, Carol. I'm sure he was just having a bad day. We are all entitled to one of those every now and then."

"I can't believe you're defending him!" She started to get up, but he grabbed her hand and pulled her back down.

"No one is purposely trying to upset you. You're just overly sensitive right now. I'm sure that the next time you run into him you'll see him in a whole new light."

"I doubt that!" She quickly stood up, then added, "Besides, he isn't someone I would ever care to run into again."

"That might be hard to do if you get the job. You may be too embarrassed to call, but they know me down at the clinic. I was the mayor, remember? I can explain..."

"Dad, stop! I won't be working with Dr. Keith Bradley. As a matter of fact, I hope I never see him again!" This time she stormed out of the room, leaving her father with a huge grin on his face.

Thankfully, she didn't see Keith Bradley at the preschool when she picked up Lizzie later that afternoon. However she had looked for his car in the pickup line. When she saw his little boy jump into a minivan much like her own, she figured it was the child's mother who was picking him up. She then felt sorry for the woman for being married to such an obstinate man.

Lizzie was so excited when she got into the van that Carol was able to shake away the bad thoughts she was having. Lizzie had been given the part of an angel in the school's Christmas pageant and began talking incessantly about it just as soon as she got into the van.

"I get to tell the shepherds that Jesus is born!" She said excitedly. "I also get to wear golden wings!"

"That's fantastic, Lizzie. You'll be a beautiful angel. I can't wait to see the play."

"I bet Daddy will…" She had forgotten again. She became silent and looked out her window.

"Daddy would have loved it, Lizzie," Carol said as she caught her daughter's eye in the rear view mirror.

"Mommy, do you think Daddy is in heaven?"

The question surprised Carol. The older Lizzie got, the more inquisitive she became.

"I know that Jesus loved Daddy very much."

"Yes, but is he in heaven? Is he watching us?"

"I believe that Daddy is resting."

"He's sleeping? Will he wake up soon?"

"Oh, Lizzie, you have so many questions that I don't have answers for." Carol's eyes filled with tears. She then attempted to change the subject. "You know who else will want to come see your play?"

"Who?"

"Papa and Nana, and of course, Blake and Zoe will want to see it, too. You have lots of family here in Snowflake Falls, Lizzie. They will all want to be there."

"Kyle gets to be a donkey. He's not happy about that because he wanted to be an angel with me."

"Who's Kyle?" She asked, thankful Lizzie was back to talking about the play.

"My new best friend. You know, he was throwing a big fit for his daddy, but you know why he was?"

"No, did he tell you why?"

"Yeah. He didn't want to go to school, but once he got there he said he was glad he came because he now has a new best friend."

"And that's you, right?"

"Yep." Lizzie grinned.

"I'm glad that you made a new friend."

"You can be friends with his daddy. Maybe he can be your new best friend, too." Lizzie nodded her head, liking that idea. "Then we can do all sorts of things together."

Carol didn't respond to that. There was no way Kyle's father would ever be her new best friend. The thought of that actually made her feel ill. She decided it was time to talk about something else. "I think Papa and Nana are going to go get a Christmas tree tonight. You'll need to take a nap when we get home so that you won't be too tired to go with them." Carol looked in the rear view mirror and saw that Lizzie had begun to pout. "No, pouting. A nap will do you some good, and when Blake gets home from school, you both can have cookies and milk."

"What time will Blake be home?"

"Around three," she answered as she drove up into the driveway. "Aunt Josie is picking him up from school."

They had lunch, then while Lizzie and Zoe took their nap, Carol searched the want ads, finding nothing she was even remotely qualified to do. She had already applied at the hospital, but hadn't heard back from them yet. She didn't want to return to the crazy hours she would have to work in a hospital setting, but at the moment she didn't think it would be any worse than working for someone like Keith Bradley.

Right at three o'clock the two boys came running into the house chattering excitedly about something. Josie followed close behind them.

"Whoa! One at a time," Carol said. "But before I hear what has you all excited, I'd like my hug, please."

Both boys gave Carol a quick hug, then began talking at the same time once again. Carol could make out something about going to some boy's house and playing in the snow. Josie finally explained that the boys had been invited over to a friend's house to play.

"I don't know, Josie. I've always made it a rule that I need to know the parents before I allow my children to have a play date."

"This is Snowflake Falls, Carol." Josie laughed. "Everyone knows everyone. Adam has been over to Bobby's house many times. His grandmother watches him and his younger brother after school. She's only lived here a couple of years, so you wouldn't know her, but trust me the boys will be perfectly safe over there."

"Are you sure?"

"Absolutely! There is nothing to worry about." She looked down at her watch. "We better get going or they won't have much time to play. So...is it okay with you?"

"I guess so," she said with a sigh. She glanced down at Blake and nodded her head. There was no way she was going to be able to say no to that happy face. She had missed that big smile of his and was glad to see that it had finally returned.

"Great! I can drop them off, but I'll need you to pick them up in a couple of hours if that's okay."

"Sure, just give me the address."

"It's just on the other side of town," she said as she wrote down the address and handed it to Carol. "Bobby's grandmother's name is Lois Hahn. You're just going to love her! She makes the best chocolate chip cookies! Since the boys are going over to play, she'll have a fresh batch made for them. Maybe she'll give you one!"

"I'm trusting you on this, Josie."

"I promise, they will be just fine. They'll have a great time."

Blake and Adam came bounding down the stairs still chattering away. Blake, who was carrying his snow pants and gloves, didn't even look at his mother when he shouted, "Bye, Mom!"

"Wait just a second, young man!" Carol called out. "Come give your mother a kiss goodbye."

Blake laughed as he jumped into his mother's arms. "I love it here, Mom! I've got so many new friends!"

"I'm glad, sweetheart. Now listen, you do whatever Mrs. Hahn says. Don't give her any trouble."

"I won't...bye, Mom!" He pulled himself out of her arms and ran with Adam out the front door.

"Five o'clock," Josie reminded Carol as she followed the boys outside.

When the time came, she had to drive through the downtown to get to Bobby's house. Though she hadn't lived in Snowflake Falls in years, she was amazed how everything had remained almost exactly the same since she was a child, including all the Christmas decorations in every store window in town.

Though the town wasn't well known by any means, it did have a reputation in the county as the place to visit during the holidays. It was like visiting a life-sized Christmas Village. She always thought it was a little over-the-top, but it did bring the tourist which helped all the small shop owners to stay in business, so she couldn't fault them for their excessive decorating. Besides, at night, with all the little twinkling lights lining the street, it looked like a Christmas card had come to life.

As she passed the bakery, she chuckled softly. Ginger Markle, the owner, had once again turned her shop into what looked just like a gingerbread house. She had worked for Ginger all throughout high school, and to this day, it was still the best job she had ever had. Working with Ginger had almost made her want to become a baker instead of a nurse. One of her fondest memories was sitting and talking with Ginger while they drank coffee and snacked on snicker doodle cookies at the end of a long shift.

Her memories suddenly filled her with regret. She wished she had been able to get Paul to bring her and the kids here during the holidays. He had always made excuses that he couldn't take off work, but was always quick to add that if he could take some time off, he wanted his vacation to be spent somewhere exotic, not some hick town in the middle of nowhere.

As she passed by the church where she had grown up going to Sunday school, she realized her father was right. She had been away from "home" for far too long. She began to sing along with the classic Christmas carol, Joy to the World, and was beginning to feel a little better...that is until she pulled up to the curb outside Mrs. Hahn's house.

The boys were playing outside without their coats or hats on. The only one dressed appropriately was the man playing with them. "Excuse me! What is going on here?" Carol yelled just as soon as she jumped out of the van. Since she was wearing her boots, she stomped through the snow in the front yard where they were playing. Before she reached them, a snowball came flying in her direction, hitting her smack dab in the face. The shock of it caused her to fall backward into the snow.

"Oops!" The man laughed as he rushed over to help her up. He reached out a hand which she immediately swatted away.

"I can get up by myself!" It took her a few tries, but she finally made it to her feet.

As their eyes met, Carol couldn't believe who she was seeing...yet again! "You've got to be kidding me!"

"Hey, good to see you again." He grinned. He stared at her for a few moments, then reached out his hand and gently ran his fingers through her snow dampened hair.

Carol gasped at his touch. She couldn't seem to catch her breath as his fingers continued to move through her hair. Finally, she abruptly pushed his hand away. "What are you doing?" She harshly whispered because she couldn't seem to find her voice.

"You have snow in your hair, I was just...never mind." He sighed.

"What are you doing here?" She asked rather angrily.

"I live here."

"I thought this was Bobby's grandmother's house."

"It is…we live with my mother-in-law."

"You're Bobby's father?"

"Yes, I have two boys, Kyle and Bobby."

"I see…Well, Bobby's dad, I am Blake's mother. Why doesn't he have his coat on? It's freezing out here!"

"It's not that cold, besides the boys were all sweating with their coats on. Your son alone has on three layers of clothes. Trust me, he's fine without his coat on."

"No, he isn't. He'll catch a cold!" She rushed over to where the coats were piled and pulled out her son's. "Blake, come put this on right now!"

"But Mr. Bradley said I didn't have to wear it."

"Well, Mr. Bradley doesn't get to decide that!"

Blake dropped his head as he slowly made his way to where his mother was standing. She handed him his coat and stood there making sure that he put it on. She then called Adam over. "You, too, young man!" Adam obeyed, but did so with a "Hmph!"

"Now, come on you two, it's time to go home. Go get in the van."

"Listen, don't leave upset. No harm was done. The boys had a great time."

"I'm sure they did. It's always fun when you don't have any *adult* supervision." She was sure to look him straight in the eye when she accentuated the word *adult* in a loud voice.

"What? Of course they had adult supervision. I've been out here playing with them the entire time. Like I said, I'm Bobby's father."

"Yes, I got that, but I would like to remind you that you are not Blake's father. If you wanted your son to catch a cold, that's fine. However, you shouldn't have made the negligent assumption that other parents would be okay with that."

"I know that I'm not Blake's father, but I just bet that his father would be a bit more reasonable about this!" He snapped.

"You don't know anything about his father," she barely whispered, too upset to speak.

"Yeah, well, I'd much rather deal with him than his crazy wife!" He then looked over at his son and said, "Bobby, go over to the van and say goodbye to your friends."

After Bobby had said his goodbyes, Carol started the engine and was just about to pull away when she heard a tapping at her window. She jumped as she turned her head and found Keith standing at her door motioning for her to row down the window. She did so, because she thought he was going to apologize. Instead, he simply handed her the boys' hats. He then quickly turned and walked away.

Carol was outraged as she drove to Josie's house. She was just going to drop Adam off, but she then decided she better go inside to let her sister know what had happened. She was pleased to find that heir cousin, Thomasina, was there with her husband Mike, the head surgeon at the hospital in town.

"Carol! I've been wanting to come see you!" Thomasina said as she embraced her cousin.

"Hi, Tommi! I was going to stop by your pottery shop soon. I've been dying to see it."

"Yes, definitely stop by. We can have lunch or something." She turned toward her husband. "You remember, Mike, don't you?"

"Of course. Hi, Mike. It's good to see you."

"It's good to see you, too. I can't believe this is Blake." He reached out his hand and rumpled the hair on top of Blake's head. "I can see you've grown into a fine looking young man."

Blake smiled at that. He liked being called a man. "Mom, can I go see Adam's room?"

"Sure, but just for a few minutes." After the boys were out of hearing range, Carol moved a bit closer to Josie and in a quiet voice said, "If Adam gets sick, I thought you should know that it's all Bobby's father's fault!"

"Keith?" Josie said with a look of shock on her face.

"Are you talking about Keith Bradley?" Mike asked.

"Yes, Dr. Keith Bradley!" She said angrily. "The town's pediatrician who obviously knows absolutely nothing about children!"

"Carol, what happened? I don't think I've ever seen you this upset." Josie reached out and began to rub her sister's arm trying to help calm her down.

"He let the boys play in the snow without their hats and coats on."

"Oh, that's no big deal," Josie said. "I'm sure..."

"Also," Carol interrupted, "he has a son in preschool, too. We met this morning after he nearly rear ended me with that ridiculous sports car he drives! He's such a child!"

Josie opened her mouth to speak, thinking Carol was finished with her tirade, but she was only getting started. "He is the most obstinate, arrogant, and insufferable man I have ever met. He's so rude and..."

"Keith Bradley?" Mike asked again, confused by Carol's behavior.

"Yes! He's a horrible man! Why do all of you look so surprised by this?"

Thomasina chuckled, "Carol, Keith Bradley is one of Mike's closest friends. Mike was instrumental in getting Keith to come to Snowflake Falls to work at the clinic. I'm surprised by what you're saying because he happens to be one of the nicest men I've ever met. He would never do anything to hurt the boys. I can't believe you think he's so awful. As a matter of fact, the two of you have a lot in common."

"I seriously doubt that!" Carol turned her head and looked accusingly at her sister, "I thought you said a sweet, little old grandmother named Lois Hahn would be watching the boys."

"Lois is Keith's mother-in-law. Carol...Keith is a single father, raising two little boys on his own. He's had it really rough."

"It figures. I suppose his wife left him. He's so..."

"Yes, as a matter of fact, his wife did leave him," Mike said. "She died two years ago."

49

Chapter Five

Keith Bradley stormed inside his home, slamming the door behind him. He was furious by the accusation that he was a bad father. What was her problem anyway? Ever since his encounter with that woman earlier in the day, he had been all out of sorts and could never seem to get back on track. He didn't care how beautiful she was, that didn't give her the right to act like a spoiled brat!

He angrily exhaled before entering the kitchen to check on his mother-in-law. He then forced a smile on his face, knowing she would hound him about what was wrong if she thought he was upset about something.

"Was that Bobby slamming the door like that? I've had to talk to him about that a time or two," Lois said as she bent down to pull a tray of cookies out of the oven.

Keith didn't answer the question, instead he tried to quickly change the subject. "It smells good in here." He reached for a cookie, but got his hand swatted.

"You'll spoil your dinner! Besides, these cookies are for Bobby's friends to take home. Is Blake's mother here yet? Josie said she would be picking the boys up about this time. She just arrived in town, so I wanted to give her a tin of cookies to welcome her."

"She's already come and gone," he said, trying hard not to sound annoyed, though inwardly he was still fuming.

"Really? That's too bad, I wanted to meet her. I hear that she is just a lovely woman. I guess she grew up in this town. She was crowned Miss Corn Queen at the Harvest Fest, don't ya know?" She giggled. "I haven't seen her yet, but I hear she is a real beauty. What did you think?"

"I didn't notice," he lied.

"You didn't, huh?" She grinned as she turned to look at him. "Josie said that after high school she moved to Chicago to go to nursing school. That's where she met her husband."

"I wonder why she moved back here."

"Oh, that...well, she became a single mother a year ago. She actually has three kids. The youngest is only two years old."

"Did she get a divorce?" That seemed like the most obvious answer to Keith, thinking she was probably really difficult to live with.

"No, Keith," she said as she turned to look at him. "She's a widow. Her husband died in a car accident a little over a year ago. The poor thing was left without a dime, that's what I heard. She was forced to move back in with her parents."

He was still stuck on what his mother had just said about her being a widow. "I guess that explains why she acts the way she does," he said under his breath hoping she wouldn't hear. He had forgotten, however, about his mother-in-law's extra sensitive hearing aids.

"Oh?" Lois faced him with raised eyebrows. "How does she act?"

"She's just a bit...oh, I don't know, cranky. I understand, though, I think I was a little on edge that first year after Kim had died."

"A little? You were more than just a little on edge! You were a complete wreck! You were also overly protective of the boys. You kept checking on them all night long."

"I did that?" He chuckled.

"Yes, you did. You weren't quiet about it, either. Those poor boys would wake up every time you opened the door. Remember how squeaky that door was?"

"I was always so afraid I was going to do something wrong. I guess I still am a little."

"I know, but you're a wonderful father. The boys adore you...and so do I." Lois wrapped her arms around his waist and gave him a tight squeeze. "You know, it might do you both some good to be friends."

"With who? Blake's mom?"

"Her name is Carol. I'm sure that she is probably in need of some support from someone who's been there and knows that it takes time to heal after losing a spouse."

"Oh, man!" Keith grimaced as he ran his fingers through his hair.

"What?"

"I said a terrible thing to her." He cringed as he remembered the expression she gave him when he told her that Blake's father would have been more reasonable.

"Well, what do I always tell the boys?"

"That an apology goes a long way to mend all sorts of hurt."

"I'm glad you remembered. I can get her phone number from Josie so that you can call her...preferably as soon as possible. You don't want to let the sun go down on your angry words."

"Yeah, if you could get her number, I'll call her this evening…or better yet, since I know where her parents live, I can stop by and apologize with a plate of those cookies."

"That would be a wonderful thing to do." Lois said as she patted his arm.

"Do you think she'll forgive me?"

"Of course, she will! Who could resist that handsome face of yours!" She reached up and pinched his cheek.

"All right, well, I guess I'll stop by this evening. Do you think I should call first and let her know that I'm coming?"

"Um…" Lois smiled as she shook her head. "I think I would just stop by unannounced. If you call first, it might give her a chance to run away."

"Wait, you just said she wouldn't be able to resist this face?"

"I know, but…just in case she's still angry with you. Women can hold on to things."

"Why would you think she's angry with me?"

Lois shrugged her shoulders before saying, "Oh, I'm guessing by the way you slammed the front door that you were angry with her as well...and for the record, I agree with her. The boys should have kept their hats and coats on." She gave him a little nob before she began stacking cookies into a metal tin. "Oh, by the way, don't make plans for this weekend."

"Why not?"

"We've been invited to Floyd and Nova's Christmas party."

"I know, but I really need to spend some time with the boys."

"They're invited, too. I guess it's going to be quite the party. I hear Floyd might even play Santa Claus for the kids."

"Let's see how this week goes. It's only Monday and I'm already exhausted."

"You need to slow down a bit, Keith. I know this time of year brings back a lot of memories for you. Maybe this year, you should take the day off and spend it with the boys doing something fun." She then looked heavenward and shook her head. "It's so hard to believe it will be two years next week."

"I know." He also shook his head. "I miss her like crazy. I suppose you're probably right. I should just take it easy this month and focus on the boys."

"Now, about that other thing," Lois said as she handed him the tin of cookies. "I feel I need to remind you to be nice. She's vulnerable right now."

"Don't worry, I'm always nice." He grinned while he reached around her and took one of the cookies still on the tray and quickly plopped it inside his mouth. He then hurried out of the kitchen before she was able to swat him with her spatula.

He laughed when he heard her call out, "Keith Bradley, I mean it! Be nice!"

Chapter Six

"Are you sure you don't want to come with us. You used to love to help pick out the tree," Abby said, hoping to change Carol's mind.

"Zoe's not feeling well. You can take Blake and Lizzie, though. I think I'm going to just put Zoe to bed early."

"You should make an appointment for Zoe at the clinic. I can call tomorrow if you want."

"I'll do it. She's due for a well baby check anyway, and Lizzie is going to need her immunizations."

"Okay, well...I guess we'll go then. Blake! Lizzie! Papa is already in the car waiting for us," Abby called out. Within seconds the two came running to the front door overly excited about getting a Christmas tree.

"Can I help chop it down?" Blake asked.

Abby began to laugh. "You'll have to ask Papa about that. I don't know if he'll trust you with a saw." When she saw the frown on his face, she added, "But...you and Lizzie can pick out the tree."

"We can get any tree we want?" Lizzie asked.

"Well, it can't be too tall. It has to fit inside the house." Abby laughed again as she took each of their hands and led them out to the garage. "We'll be about an hour or so," she said to Carol as she walked out the door.

After Carol put Zoe to bed, she went downstairs to read a book, something she hadn't been able to do in a very long time. However, just as soon as she sat down, the doorbell rang. She groaned as she stood back up. After the day she had had, she wasn't in the mood for visiting with anyone which obviously showed on her face when she opened the door.

"Don't you ever smile?" Keith asked as soon as he saw her sour face.

"What are you doing here?" She asked angrily. "And How did you know where I live?"

"Well, first of all, I stopped by because I wanted to talk to you about something, and as to your second question, I knew where you lived because this is a small town...need I say more?" He looked at her with a slight grin on his face.

"What do you want?" She said rudely as she pulled her sweater closer together, shivering from the cold air. "And make it quick. It's freezing out here."

"I come bearing gifts." He smiled as he held out the tin of cookies. "My mother-in-law has perfected the art of making chocolate chip cookies."

She was hesitant to take the tin from him. She felt like there had to be some sort of catch behind the gift.

"It's okay. It's just cookies." He extended his arm further so that the tin was closer to her reach.

She sighed heavily, causing a smoke-like effect from her frozen breath. "Thank you," she said as she took the tin. She then took a step back into the house and reached for the door to shut it.

"Wait! I wanted to...I mean I think we got off to a bad start."

"Ya think?" She said sarcastically.

"Do you suppose I could come in? You're right, it's freezing out here." He slid his numb hands deep inside his coat pockets.

"No," she answered as she reached for the door again.

"Are you serious?"

"Yes, I'm very serious. I'm not letting a stranger come inside my house."

"We're hardly strangers...but to make it official…" He pulled a hand out of his pocket and extended it toward her. "Hello, my name is Keith Bradley. It's nice to make your acquaintance."

Though she looked at his hand, she didn't take it, nor did she reply. She simply gathered her sweater even tighter against herself and shook her head.

It was difficult for him not to show how annoyed he was by her behavior, but he kept his voice as calm as possible when he said, "The proper response is to take my hand and shake it while introducing yourself to me."

"Fine, my name is Carol, and...you're still not coming in." She glared at him this time.

"Listen, I came over to apologize. I didn't realize that you had a good reason to behave the way that you did today. I understand…" He stopped himself when he saw the shocked expression on her face and thought that maybe he had taken the wrong approach.

"I have not been behaving badly...you have!"

He reached up and rubbed his temples, feeling a headache coming on. He wasn't sure if it was from the cold air, or from trying to talk to a very stubborn woman. "Let me start over. This morning, I was in a hurry and a bit impatient. I'm very sorry how I treated you. This afternoon I felt like you overreacted, and so I said some things I regret saying. I didn't know at the time that your husband had died."

"My husband being dead has nothing to do with this. Yes, you were impatient...and very rude! For heaven's sake, you lifted me completely off the floor. I was so…" She shook her head not wanting to tell him how humiliated he had made her feel. "Then, I had to find out that the job that I desperately needed is a position working with you! I didn't think the day could get any worse until I picked up Blake and Adam and there you were once again letting them play in the cold without their coats on!"

"Look, I said I was sorry."

"Okay, well...whatever. I need to go." She took a few steps back and began to shut the door. He, however, took a few steps forward and caught the door with his hand, preventing it from closing.

"What are you doing?" She snapped angrily.

"I'm waiting."

"For what?" She practically shouted.

"I'm waiting for you to apologize to me."

Carol's eyes widened in shock as she once again shouted, "For what?"

"For one, walking out of an interview that I had to change my schedule for in order to be there, and then later for basically accusing me of being a bad father."

"Well, if the shoe fits…" She started to slam the door again, but it wouldn't budge against his strong arm.

"I am not a bad father!" He shouted back, then immediately felt bad when he saw tears spring to her eyes. "Sorry, I shouldn't have yelled."

Carol could hear Zoe crying in the background. "Now look what you did!" She hurried up the steps toward the room Zoe was in, leaving the front door wide open.

Keith took advantage of the situation and walked inside the house, closing the door behind him. He then walked into the living room and sat down on the couch to wait for her to come back downstairs.

He could hear her softly singing a lullaby through the speaker of the child monitor sitting on the coffee table. It was one his wife had sung to their boys when they were babies. Hearing the sweet melody caused his heart to tighten. He tried not to let himself think too much about his wife this time of year. The sadness was consuming at times. Knowing he needed to be focused at work, and especially at home raising his boys, he tried not to dwell on his grief. However, the sweet melody coming over the speaker made it difficult not to think about his wife. He felt tears begin to form in his eyes, and for just a moment he closed them and tried to see her face.

Carol finally managed to get Zoe back to sleep. She then tiptoed out of the room and went back downstairs. She stopped at the bottom of the steps and began to massage her neck in an attempt to ease the tension she was feeling. She felt her heart begin to pound against her chest and her throat became constricted. She took huge gulps of breath as if she were drowning. She felt the panic begin to rise in her once again. She had dealt with this off and on for over a year now, but she had thought she was getting better. *God, please, help me,* she prayed just before she slumped down onto the bottom step and began to cry.

Keith had a view of the steps from where he was sitting. He knew she hadn't noticed him yet, but he had been watching her and saw a woman who was tired and weary. He knew exactly what she was going through, and he also knew exactly what she needed.

He quietly stood up and walked over to the staircase. He then reached down and gently pulled her up off the step and into his arms. He thought she might resist his embrace when she looked up into his eyes, clearly surprised to see him standing there. They stood that way for several moments, just looking deep into each others' eyes, both seeing the depth of sorrow they possessed as well as the longing to be free of it.

He wasn't sure what she was going to do, but he never expected for her to slowly move her hands up across his chest. She then wrapped them securely around his neck as she leaned her head in the crook of his neck, pressing her cheek against the spot where his pulse was beating wildly.

It was all the encouragement he needed to pull her closer, wrapping his arms tighter around her slim waist. "It's going to be okay," he whispered. He placed his chin against the top of her head, breathing in the soft scent of lavender from her shampoo. A peaceful quiet washed over them like a refreshing shower on a warm summer's day. Neither spoke because, at the moment, no words were needed. As they clung to each other, their broken hearts began to mend...only bits and pieces of it, but it was a beginning they both had been longing for.

"Carol," Keith finally spoke in a whisper. "I…"

The front door slammed opened with the sound of excited children instantly filling the quiet room. It was followed by a burst of cold air which quickly brought them back to reality.

"Shhh! You two will wake up your sister," Abby said. "Your mother will be so…" She stopped and gasped. "Oh… Carol…I…" Abby was stunned to see her daughter in the arms of Keith Bradley.

"Well, now, what do we have here?" Magnus grinned. "Nice to see you, Keith. I see you've met our daughter, Carol."

"Mr. Bradley!" Blake said cheerfully. "Is Bobby here?" He searched the room looking for his new friend.

Keith slowly removed his arms from around Carol's waist then nervously ran his hand through his hair a few times, trying to figure out how to best handle the awkward situation. "No, he's home. Lois made cookies and um…"

"Yes," Carol also ran her hands through her hair, knowing it must be all disheveled. "I was just thanking him…" She stopped herself from saying anything more, realizing that no one would believe what they had witnessed was a "thank you" hug. "Um...You guys are home early."

"The kids picked out the first tree they saw," Magnus said as he carried the tree over to the large picture window in the family room. "I think it's a good one. What do you think?"

"It's perfect." Carol did her best to smile.

There were several seconds of awkward silence before Keith finally said, "Well, I guess I better be getting home." He stepped away from Carol and walked over to the couch to get his jacket. "The boys are needing a bath and…" He grabbed his coat then looked over at the tree. "That is a nice tree. It reminds me I better get one soon or the boys will be after me."

"It was good to see you, Keith. We missed you at church last Sunday," Magnus said.

"Lois wasn't feeling well. I hate to leave her when she's under the weather like that."

"Completely understood. I hope she is feeling better now."

"She is." He nervously rubbed his hands together as if they were cold, when they were actually the exact opposite. He briefly looked back at Carol and smiled as he waved a quick goodbye. He then made his way to the front door, hoping to make his escape. He shut the door behind him and walked as fast as he could down the icy sidewalk out to his car. He was almost there when he heard Carol call his name.

"Keith! Wait a second," she called out as she hurried down the walkway toward him. "I…back there…" She turned her head to look back at the house. "I was…overwhelmed...and you were there, and...well, you know…"

"Yeah…" He didn't know what to say either because frankly, he wasn't sure what had just transpired between them. He just knew that he had wanted to remain in her arms forever.

"So...um...thanks again for the cookies."

"Lois wanted to welcome you back to Snowflake Falls."

"Lois, she's your mother-in-law?"

"Yeah, she was living with us before my wife died. She was going to go move in with her other daughter, but the boys had become so attached to her. She couldn't stand to leave them, and I really needed her help. My parents are no longer alive."

"Oh, I'm sorry to hear that...I'm also sorry about your wife."

"I'm sorry about your husband."

They stared into each other's eyes, both extremely cold, but neither wanting to be the first to say goodnight. Finally, Keith looked down at his watch. "The boys will be asking for me, so I guess I'll see you later."

"Yeah, at the preschool drop off line in the morning. I'll be sure to turn my blinker on." She smiled.

The smile caught him off guard. It seemed to light up her entire face. "Hey, I think that's first time I've seen you smile." He grinned down at her. "It looks good on you."

As Carol made her way back inside, she was still smiling, something she realized she hadn't done in a very long time.

Chapter Seven

Carol's smile had faded with morning's light. When she woke up and began the routine of getting Blake and Lizzie ready for school, she was feeling embarrassed by her behavior the night before. She couldn't remember how she had gotten into Keith's arms, but she did know that once she was there, she didn't want to leave. It had felt so good to be held like that and to believe, for even just a few moments, that everything was going to be okay just as he had whispered to her. However, as wonderful as it had been, she was determined to never allow something like that to ever happen again.

Carol had made a vow to never marry again. She had made that vow when she found a large envelope with divorce papers in Paul's desk drawer when she was packing up his things. By the date on the papers, she realized he had been thinking about leaving her long before the night he died.

Her hands had trembled uncontrollably as she read the papers citing "irreconcilable differences," meaning, that in Keith's opinion, the marriage was beyond repair. The worst of it, though, was that he was planning to file for custody of the children.

She had thrown the divorce papers in the fireplace and watched them burn. She never wanted anyone to see them and know that the girl, who had once been voted "most likely to succeed," had failed miserably in her marriage. As the flames licked at the crumpled papers, turning them to ash, it was at that moment that she vowed to never marry again. She might never be able to be a good wife, but she would give her heart and soul to being the best mother she could be. Though, right now she felt that she wasn't doing so great in that department, either. Zoe was still getting sick, Lizzie was having bad dreams, and Blake kept asking about his father. She felt torn in every direction.

Yes, she was attracted to Keith. She liked how he was both clean cut, and a little sloppy all at the same time. He dressed nice, but she had detected a few wrinkles in his shirt, and his tie was a bit lopsided. His hair was cut short, but he didn't use products in it to keep it from flying around as Paul had used. His eyes could be piercing, and yet they reflected an inner kindness that had made her heart beat like a drum when she had stared into them the night before.

Now that she wasn't angry with him, she realized that if she wasn't careful, she might just end up in love with him. It was for that reason that she purposely arrived as late as possible to drop off Lizzie in hopes that she wouldn't run into him again.

Carol's mother had insisted that after dropping off Lizzie, Carol should take a little time for herself. Since she needed to open a bank account and mail some past due bills, she decided to take her mother up on the offer to watch Zoe for her this morning.

After she finished her errands, she was going to head home but decided to stop by the bakery and have a cup of coffee and a cinnamon roll. Ginger used to say that even though her sweet rolls were bad for the figure, they were indeed very good for the soul. Carol needed that more than anything else this morning.

It was close to ten when she arrived at the bakery. She had to pick Lizzie up at noon, so she still had plenty of time to devour a cinnamon roll and chat with her old friend, Ginger.

"Why, if it isn't one of the prettiest baking assistants I ever had! Get over here and give me a hug!" Ginger said loudly just as soon as she looked up and saw Carol enter the bakery.

Ginger made her way around the counter and rushed toward Carol. Since it was close to Christmas, she had once again dressed the part of Mrs. Santa Claus. She had her white hair up in a bun on the top of her head, and wore a pair of wire-rimmed glasses. She had applied an extra coat of bright red blush and matching lipstick. She then finished the look by wearing a red, fur-lined apron.

"Oh, it's so good to see you again," she said as she wrapped her arms around Carol and squeezed her tight.

"Hi, Ginger!" Carol laughed. "You've still got the tightest hugs of anyone I know."

"Well, you know what I always say, hugs are like lemons. The tighter you squeeze the more of that delicious juice you'll get. A good hug will cure any ailment! Now then, let me take a look at you!" Ginger stepped back and spun Carol around with her hands. "You are as beautiful as ever...but way too skinny for my liking! A tray of hot fresh cinnamon rolls are about to come out of the oven. One has your name on it!"

"You must have read my mind. That's why I'm here. I was craving one of your world-famous rolls."

"Well, I hope you came to see me, too!" Ginger placed her hands on her hips and pretended to scowl. "I've missed you, young lady."

"I've missed you, too, Ginger...and yes, I also came to see you." Carol took a seat at one of the tall stools at the counter. "I'll take a cup of coffee, too. One sugar and…"

"Two creams," Ginger interrupted. "I remember just how you like your coffee." She smiled. "I'll be right back with your roll and coffee, then we can have a little chat just like old times."

While Ginger went to get her order, Carol looked around the bakery and smiled. The place hadn't changed a bit since she was a teenager. It was decorated to look like a sweet gingerbread house with cutout lollipops and gumdrops hanging from the ceiling. There were several Christmas trees around the room, all covered in colorful lights and candy shaped ornaments. The glass snowflakes hanging in the windows caused the room to sparkle with sunlight as if glitter was flying around in the air.

Ginger came from the back carrying a plate with the cinnamon roll on it in one hand, and in the other she carried a cup of coffee that still had steam rolling off the top. She was singing *We Wish You a Merry Christmas* along with the music playing in the background. As she placed the plate in front of Carol, she cheerfully said, "Here you are, hot and fresh right out of the oven!"

"Thank you, Ginger. I'm going to have to bring my kids in soon. They've never experienced this," she said as she took a huge bite out of the gooey, cinnamon roll. "Mmm! Just as I remembered!"

"Well, you know what the secret ingredient is, don't you?"

Before Carol could answer, a deep, voice behind her said, "From what I heard, a big ole' heaping spoon full of love goes into the mixing bowl before anything else."

"That's right!" Ginger giggled. "Floyd Emerson! I haven't seen you in two days. Where have you been hiding yourself?"

"Nova has banned me from having a cinnamon roll every day. She's at her little tea group right now, so she doesn't know I've gone missin'." His contagious laughter filled the bakery, causing the other customers in the room to laugh as well.

"Floyd, you probably haven't met Carol yet. She's Magnus Engles' oldest daughter. The poor thing lost her husband last year and had to come home to live with her folks just so she could get by."

"Ginger…" Carol's face turned a deep shade of red. She didn't want people feeling sorry for her, and she certainly didn't want her personal life being shared with a complete stranger.

"Oh, you poor girl! Come on, stand up," Floyd said with outstretched arms.

"What? I…"

He took both of her hands in his and slowly pulled her off the stool. He wrapped his arms around her and squeezed tight. "Your father and mother mean the world to me. Any child of theirs is like a child of mine."

Floyd was a big man in both height and width. He had a deep, southern drawl and a gap-toothed smile as big as a crescent moon. His skin was dark, which made his eyes and teeth look whiter than the snow outside. He was as lovable as a stuffed bear, though most people were a bit leery when first meeting the gregarious man…just as Carol was right now.

She was fully enveloped in his arms, with her face smashed up against his chest. At first she was tense, but it didn't take long for her to relax and just allow the hug to work its magic. Her father was right, this man's hugs were like nothing she had ever felt before.

"I'm having a big ole shindig this weekend. I told your parents to make sure to invite you and the kids to come along. Can I count on seeing you there?"

"Of course, she'll be there," Ginger answered for her. "I'm coming too. I wouldn't miss it for the world."

"Did Nova get her order in for those cinnamon cookies you make?"

"Oh, yes. You'll have enough cookies to feed a small army."

"Good, that means there will be leftovers." He laughed as he finally released Carol, giving her a soft pat on the top of her head as if she were a small child.

Carol sat back down and combed her fingers through her hair, knowing it was most likely a mess from being squished in Floyd's arms. "My father has told me about you and your family, Mr. Emerson. I'm looking forward to meeting your wife as well."

"What's this Mr. Emerson business? You can save that formality for my father. I'm just plain ole' Floyd, or you can call me Bubba, that's what all my friends call me. I reckon that you and I are going to be great friends."

Carol laughed as she nodded her head. She was pretty sure that he was right. How could anyone not be this man's friend?

"Now, what's this I hear? You're a widow? Why you can't be a day over 21!"

"She's 31!" Ginger corrected. "Her husband Paul died a year ago. It was a tragic car accident."

"Well, bless your heart. You've still got some mending to do, don't cha?"

Carol had to turn her eyes away from his penetrating stare. She felt like he could see all the way to her wounded heart.

"I'm fine, really."

Ginger and Floyd both studied her face for a while and neither liked what they saw. Ginger placed a hand over Carol's and gave it a tight squeeze. "You know, sweetheart, it's okay to not be okay."

"No, really, I'm…"

"No, you're not! I can see sadness a mile away. You've really been through something awful, haven't you?" Floyd chimed in.

Carol tried to blink the tears away, but there were just too many of them. She reached for a napkin and began to dab at her eyes.

"Oh, honey, I didn't mean to make you cry." Floyd wrapped an arm around her shoulders. "My friend, let me tell you this, God loves you dearly. He will heal that heart of yours and before you know it, he'll bring love back into your life again."

She shook her head. "No, I'm not ever going to marry again. I can't! I would just fail at it!" She didn't mean for that to slip out of her mouth, so she quickly changed the subject. "I'm so embarrassed. I keep doing this...crying around people. I wish I could…"

"Those tears won't be denied. You loved your husband, and he loved you. It makes all the sense in the world…" Ginger said lovingly.

"No," Carol interrupted. "No...it's not that. It's…"

Ginger waited for a few moments for her to continue what she was about to say. When she didn't, Floyd asked, "What are those tears about then?"

Thankfully, Carol's phone began to ring. She pulled it out of her purse and saw that her mother was calling. "Mom, is Zoe okay?"

"Hello, sweetheart. Everything is fine, it's just Harriet called the house looking for you. I guess Lizzie has a stomach ache. I can go get her…"

"That's okay. I'm just here at the bakery visiting with Ginger and Mr. Emerson...I mean Floyd." She looked over at Floyd and smiled. "I'll go pick her up."

"Well, I'm actually calling from the car. I'm on my way to the clinic. I checked Zoe's temperature, and she's running a little fever. I called the clinic and they were able to get us in right away. That hardly ever happens, so I took advantage of it. I would have called you first, but I didn't want to lose the appointment. The poor thing is tugging on her ears."

"I was afraid of that. It's probably another ear infection. I'm glad you were able to get her in. Um...how about I run over and pick up Lizzie. I'll then head to the clinic and you can take Lizzie home, and I'll stay with Zoe."

"That sounds fine. I'll let the gals at the clinic know that you're on your way."

As soon Carol hung up with her mother, she jumped down from the stool and quickly put on her coat. "Sorry, I need to leave."

"Is everything okay?" Ginger asked.

"Neither of my daughters are feeling well. I need to go pick one up from school and the other is already on her way to the clinic." She sighed. "Could you put this roll in a box for me?"

"Absolutely, and I'm going to add three more so that you can give one to each of your children."

"You don't have to do that. I can just share mine."

"Oh, hush that nonsense! They should all have their own cinnamon roll."

"Thanks, Ginger, I know they'll love it."

When Ginger left to go box up the pastries, Floyd, leaned down near her ear and quietly said, "You and your husband were having some troubles." It wasn't a question.

Carol 's eyes flew open as she turned to look at him. "How did you know that?"

"I didn't know for certain, but your reaction just now confirmed it for me. I don't think you're nursing a broken heart. I think you're dealing with some anger. I also think you need to forgive yourself. Until you do that, you won't be able to move on."

"Is that what happened to you? My father told me that you were once in prison."

"Yes, I was. That's where I met Otis, your grandfather."

"You two were friends?"

"The best of friends. He was like a father to me and helped me get through the roughest time of my life."

"He was actually my step-grandfather, but I never thought of him that way."

"That's because he loved you all as if you were blood-kin. He was a good man and never gave up on me. You see, I continued to be in prison even after I was released. I couldn't forgive myself for all that I had done. Your grandfather continued to share God's Word with me about the forgiveness Jesus so freely offers. It took me a while, but I finally figured it out. Now…" He placed his large hand on her shoulder as he looked directly into her eyes. "I don't know what went on between you and your husband, but hangin' on to what once was doesn't get you anywhere. You need to be able to let it go."

"I wish I could…"

Floyd was going to say something else, but Ginger walked back into the room. She handed the box of rolls to Carol, then said,"You know, I was just thinking, I suspect you'll be visiting with Dr. Bradley. He's a widower too...a very handsome one at that. I think the two of you..."

"Okay, well, it was good to see you again, Ginger," Carol said hastily, cutting her off. She was all too familiar with Ginger's matchmaking attempts. She turned to Floyd and reached out her hand to shake his, "It was very nice to meet you, Floyd."

"Put that hand away!" He grabbed her and smashed her hard against his chest again. "I'll be seeing you this weekend. I want to meet those kids of yours...I know someone else who wants to meet them, too!" He held on to his belly with both hands and gave a loud, "Ho! Ho! Ho!"

Carol smiled as she walked away. "I'll think about it," she called out.

"No...I think you'll be there...you and I are friends now. You don't say no to a friend, now do ya?" He grinned.

"I suppose you don't." She walked outside and headed toward her car. It wasn't until she snapped the buckle in place that she realized that her smile had returned.

Chapter Eight

Carol knew as soon as she picked up Lizzie that she wasn't sick at all. Harriet explained that she had gotten into a squabble with one of the other little girls. Apparently, Lizzie was told that she was dumb because she didn't have a father. Harriet had done her best to resolve the situation, but when Lizzie had laid her head on her desk, pretending to be sick, she figured she better give Carol a call.

"Of course, you have a father, Lizzie. He loved you very much," Carol said on their way to the clinic.

"But he left and isn't coming back. I don't want to be dumb anymore."

"You're not dumb. That little girl didn't know what she was talking about."

"But Mommy, when is Daddy coming back?"

She looked at her daughter through the rearview mirror and could see tears filling her eyes. "Honey, don't cry." She didn't know what else to say. "Hey, listen, we're going to stop by the clinic where Zoe is. Nana will bring you home, and I'll ask her to be sure to give you a cookie before your nap today. How does that sound?"

"I don't want a cookie," she huffed as she turned her head and looked out the window.

When Carol arrived at the clinic, her mother and Zoe had already been called back to the waiting room. When she stopped at the reception area, Amanda, the clinic administrator, was in the front office. When she saw Carol, she stepped up to the window so she could speak quietly. "Mrs. Brunswick, I was hoping I'd see you again. Are you okay? You left the interview so abruptly, I was afraid we had said something to upset you."

"No...I apologize. I..." Carol didn't know what to say so she did her best to change the subject. "Would it be all right if I go back where my daughter is? She's here with my mother."

"Of course, just go through that door." She pointed to the door leading back to the examining rooms.

"Thank you," Carol said as she took Lizzie by the hand and hurried through the door. As soon as she opened the door to the examining rom, Zoe's face lit up with a smile. She then reached her arms up in the air for her mother to pick her up. "Mama, up!"

"Hey, there, Zo-zo." She pulled her daughter into her arms and immediately felt her forehead. "You do feel warm. Did a nurse take her temperature yet?"

"Yes, it's getting higher," Abby said.

"Oh, Zoe." She sighed. "I hope the doctor can make this all better for you."

Just then they heard a soft tap on the door before it opened. "So, who do we have here?" Keith entered the room still looking down at the chart. "So which one of you is Miss Zoe Brunswick?" He looked up and gazed across the room, first at Lizzie, then Zoe, finally stopping at Carol. He immediately began to smile. "Hey, I missed you at the preschool line this morning."

When her heart skipped a beat, she quickly reminded herself, *I'm not ever getting married again.* She turned her head slightly so that she wouldn't have to look him in the eye. "Thank you for seeing us on such short notice, Dr. Bradley. My mother is the one that made the appointment...so…"

Keith looked at her curiously and realized she was feeling uncomfortable. He reached out and touched her arm, repeating the same words from the night before. "It's going to be okay." He then shook Abby's hand. "Good to see you again, Abby."

"You as well. I hope you'll be able to help our sweet Zoe." She reached down and took Lizzie by the hand. "Carol, I'm going to head home with Lizzie now."

"Thanks for all your help, Mom. She's fine by the way. I think she just needs some hugs, right Lizzie?"

"I just baked a batch of cookies. Maybe Mommy will let you have one before lunch." Abby looked at Carol for approval.

"If you can get her to eat one. She said she didn't…"

"I changed my mind!" Lizzie finally smiled as she took her grandmother's hand and walked with her out of the room.

Keith looked at Carol again and reached out his arms. "May I take her?"

"I don't think she'll…" To Carol's surprise, Zoe happily reached her arms out to him. He pulled her close as she wrapped her arms around his neck and laid her head on his shoulder.

"Okay, Miss Zoe, let's see if we can help make you feel better."

Carol watched with interest as Keith began to examine her daughter. He was so gentle with her and spoke in a soft voice. It didn't take long at all before he had Zoe's full attention. He even managed to make her giggle while he was checking her ears.

After he had thoroughly examined her ears, nose, and throat he gathered Zoe back into his arms. "You've got yourself a real sweetheart with this cutie pie!" He swept her hair away from her face and tucked it behind her ears. "Unfortunately, she has a double ear infection. I also want to run a test on her throat just to rule out strep."

"She's never had a throat swab done. I don't know if you'll be able to get a sample," Carol said. She reached her arms out for Zoe to come to her, but she just shook her head and clung tighter to Keith's neck.

"I'm usually pretty good at getting in there, but I may need your help holding her down."

"Okay, well, let's get this over with," Carol said anxiously. As a nurse, she had helped take care of lots of children and never once flinched if they got upset. However, with her own children it was the exact opposite.

Carol was fully prepared for the fit she was certain Zoe would make, but, once again to her surprise, Keith didn't need her help at all. He explained what he was going to do in the most kid friendly way. "Okay, Miss Zoe, I need to check to see if there are any icky bugs in your throat. I need you to open real wide." Zoe seemed to understand and opened her mouth as wide as she could. He was able to get his sample before Zoe even knew what had happened.

"Miss Zoe, you are a dream child. I've never had it that easy!" He held out his hand for a high five but received her outstretched arms wanting him to pick her up again. "Come here, sweetie." He pulled her into his arms again and began to gently pat her back. "I'll send a prescription over to the pharmacy," he said, looking at Carol.

Carol held out her arms for Zoe to come to her, but once again she wouldn't budge. "Sorry, I think she's smitten with you."

Keith just laughed and said, "The feeling is mutual." He opened the door and waited for Carol to go first. "I'll walk with you all back to the reception area." As they walked out of the room, he added, "I want you to make an appointment for two weeks from now. We'll check her ears again after she's gone through the full ten days of antibiotics. Call me, though, if she doesn't seem to be getting better after a few days."

Carol looked up at Keith and smiled. "Thank you again for seeing her today, Dr. Bradley."

"I was happy to…and it's Keith, by the way. I'll call you this afternoon with the strep results."

"Okay. Well…Dr…Keith," she smiled up at him. "I guess I'll talk to you later then."

"Carol...I was wondering…" He hesitated a little as if he was unsure of himself. "Would you..."

"Dr. Bradley," a nurse said as she approached them. "You have a call on line three."

"Sure, um..." He handed Zoe over to Carol and said, "Goodbye sweetheart. You feel better, okay?"

"Bye-bye," Zoe said as she waved her hand.

When Carol arrived back at home, she was feeling nervous. She wasn't exactly sure why, but she figured it had something to do with Keith. She didn't want to like him, but she was finding it harder and harder not to. Besides being very handsome, he was an amazing doctor. She couldn't believe how Zoe had taken to him. She had never done that with any of her other doctors.

"We're home," Carol called out as soon as she walked through the door.

"What's the verdict?" Abby asked as she and Lizzie walked out of the kitchen.

"Double ear infection." Carol sighed.

"Oh, my poor girl," Abby said as she reached out her arms to take Zoe. "Do you have a prescription?"

"Yes." Carol pulled out a bag from her purse. "Would you mind giving Zoe her first dose. I'll start on some lunch for the girls."

"Lunch is all ready. Lizzie helped me make sandwiches."

"Me and Zoe get peanut butter and jelly! I spread the jelly myself!" Lizzie said proudly.

"That's wonderful, Lizzie. Zoe may not feel like eating, but we'll see if she'll try." Carol then looked at her mother and sighed. "It's been a long morning."

"Are you all right, sweetheart? You look worried. I'm sure Zoe will be just fine."

"I know...I just have a lot on my mind."

"Do you want to talk about it?"

Carol shook her head. "I don't want to burden you with all my problems."

"Nothing you say or do is a burden to me. I understand that this is a very difficult time for you. I want to be able to help in any way that I can."

"I know that you do, and I'm very grateful for all the help that you and Dad have been with the kids. Unfortunately, you won't be able to help me find a job. Here is it two weeks before Christmas, and I have to decide between buying gifts for the children or making my car payment. Next month, if I'm still out of work, it will be deciding between the car payment or paying the car insurance. After that, I won't have enough money to decide anything."

"Your father and I will take care of those bills for you. I don't know why you worry."

"I thought I made it clear that if I came home, I was not going to be taken care of. I have to do this on my own. I can't let you or anyone else be responsible for me."

"You've always been very independent. It was always so hard for you to let us do anything for you, even when you were a child."

"Independence is not a bad thing, Mom."

"I know, but right now you are struggling. It's also okay to let others help you."

"It's hard for me," she said with a sigh. "I don't know why."

"Everything will be okay. Besides, you may get that job you interviewed for."

"I doubt that. I walked out of the interview."

"You did what?"

"Sorry, I thought Dad would have told you. I was scared and stupid. I didn't think I could work that close with Dr. Bradley."

"The position was working with Keith?"

"Yes, it was. He and I got off to a bad start, but last night...well, you know...and now seeing how wonderful he was with Zoe...I'm just confused."

"Carol, he's a good man."

"I know he is!" She responded loudly, which caused Zoe to pout. Carol ran her hand through Zoe's fine hair. "I'm sorry, sweetheart."

"From what I witnessed last night, it seems you might actually like him," Abby said with slight grin.

"It wouldn't matter if I did because he would never like me. I'm a terrible person. I can't do anything right!" She slumped down onto the couch, pushing her hands deep into her eye sockets desperately trying to avoid crying yet again.

"Oh, honey," Abby said as she put Zoe down before sitting next to her daughter on the couch. "Where in the world is all this coming from? You are not a terrible person. You are an amazing mother. You…"

"Stop! I'm not! Look at Zoe! She's sick again. I must be doing something horribly wrong!"

Zoe started to cry when she saw how distressed her mother was. "See…all I do is make her cry!"

Abby picked up Zoe and began to pat her back to try and comfort her. "I'm going to go give Zoe the antibiotics, then I'm going to feed her and Lizzie some lunch. I'll put them both down for a nap after they eat. I want you to stay right there and try to get a little rest."

"I'm sorry, Mom. I'm just so tired."

"I know you are, that's why I want you to rest."

"No, I should go take care of the girls." She started to stand up.

"No, you shouldn't." Abby said. "You need to listen to your mother."

Carol wanted to be stubborn about this, but she was exhausted both physically and mentally, so she did as her mother said. However, just as soon as she closed her eyes, her cellphone began to ring. "Hello," she answered.

"Hi there, this is Keith."

"How did you get my number…oh, from the clinic, right?"

"Yes, I wanted to call with the results of the strep test. It looks like Zoe has strep throat as well as the ear infections. The antibiotics I gave you should take care of both. Also, I forgot to ask earlier, is she getting frequent ear infections?"

"Yes, I've lost count of how many she's had."

"It probably time to think about having a tympanoplasty done for Zoe."

"You're talking ear tube surgery?"

"It's a simple procedure. I do them all the time. We can wait until she's feeling better, maybe after Christmas."

"Okay, well, we can discuss it at our next appointment."

"Sounds good, um...before you hang up, I was wondering if I might call you sometime?"

"Call me? For what?"

"Coffee, dinner, whatever you're comfortable with."

"I don't know." She lifted her hand to her heart and could feel how rapidly it was beating.

"That's not really an answer." He chuckled.

"It's the only one I have, though."

"How does this weekend sound?"

"For what?"

"For dinner."

"I already have plans this weekend."

"Okay, how about one day next week?"

"I don't know, Keith. I just need more time."

"How much time do you need? I'm a patient man."

Carol didn't respond to that, instead she said, "I need to go check on the girls. Thanks for calling."

"Don't hang up, Carol."

"Keith...I've got to go."

"I just want you to know that I'm scared to. I haven't asked anyone out since Kim died."

There was a long pause, with both wondering what the other was thinking. Finally, Carol spoke just a little louder than a whisper, "Why me?"

"Because last night when I held you in my arms, I felt alive for the first time in…I don't know how long. I think you felt it, too."

She nodded her head, silently agreeing with him. However, *I'm never getting married again* echoed over and over again in her mind.

"Carol? Are you still there?"

"I've gotta go." This time she hung up before he could say another word.

Chapter Nine

"Winslow! Would you look at this!" Cecily yelled as she came through the front door holding a letter in her hand. "She didn't even have the decency to call us, or to come over and let us say a proper goodbye to the children!"

"What's got you so upset, dear?" Winslow put down the paper he had been reading and looked up at his wife.

"This!" She waved the letter in her hand. "She's left Chicago!"

"I assume that you're referring to Carol."

"Did you know about this?"

"Yes, she called to let us know she was leaving a few weeks ago."

"When did she call?"

"Don't you remember? She invited us over, but you feigned a headache."

"I did not pretend to be ill. You know I get migraines! I feel one coming on right now!" She huffed angrily.

"Yes, dear…I know." He said sarcastically. "You always seem to get them. Especially, when Carol invited us over."

"So, you knew that she was leaving?" She had a look of outrage on her face as she sat down at the table next to her husband.

"Yes, I knew. I stopped by to say goodbye to her and the children, and as usual, made excuses why you couldn't be there."

"Winslow! I can't believe you kept this from me. You should have talked to me about this."

"Well, I know how it upsets you, dear…and to be frank, I wanted to spare myself a headache from hearing you carry on about it. Besides, Carol told me that she would write a letter to you. I figured we could talk about it when you got the letter. Now that you have it there in your hand, we can talk about it if that's what you'd like to do." He waited a few seconds for her to say

79

something. When all she did was sit there with her mouth opened, shaking her head in unbelief, he picked up the paper again and began reading where he had left off.

Cecily reached for the paper and pulled it back down so that she could see her husband's face. "I don't know how you can be so nonchalant about all this! How could she take our grandchildren away from us?" Her eyes filled with tears. "We'll never see them again!"

"Cecily, dear, that's what airplanes are for. We are retired. We can go see them whenever we want. Carol made that clear to me. She still wants us to be a part of their lives."

"I will not step foot in that ridiculous little...town, city...Oh, I don't know what you call it!"

"Well, then you probably won't ever see our grandchildren if that's how you feel." He lifted the paper, hiding his face once more from his wife.

"Winslow!" She huffed in frustration. "We have to do something."

He sighed heavily, regretting that he didn't accept the invitation to go have coffee with one of his golf buddies this morning. He was a bit under the weather and was hoping for a peaceful morning at home. He peered over the top of the paper. "What do you have in mind?"

"I don't know...I just...maybe we can file for custody."

Winslow slowly folded the paper in half, then loudly slapped it on the table. He wanted his wife to know he had had enough. "We'll do no such thing! Carol is a good mother. No court would take her children away from her."

"She's not...she's…" She stopped when Winslow held up his hand.

"Don't start that nonsense again. I've never understood why you didn't like the poor thing. She's as cute as button, and she was always so friendly to us."

"Carol?"

"Yes, Carol," Winslow said, becoming agitated with his wife. "Who else are we talking about right now?"

"She was not friendly to me at all. It was obvious that she was jealous of my relationship with Paul!"

"I don't think so, dear." He pushed the chair back then stood to his feet. "I believe it was the exact opposite." He was done with this conversation. He had had it too many times before and had grown weary of it.

"I was not jealous of her! It's just she never liked me because Paul was so fond of me!" She began to cry, hoping to gain some sympathy from her husband. Usually it worked, but this time Winslow walked out of the room, leaving her alone at the table.

Still grasping the letter in her hand, she looked down at it and once again read what Carol had written to her. *Dear Cecily, I'm sorry that I wasn't able to see you before I moved to Snowflake Falls. It's been a very long and difficult year for me and the children. Moving back home with my parents was the only option I had. I want you and Winslow to know that you are always welcome to come visit. As I have said many times before, I am so sorry that Paul died. His absence has left a huge hole in my heart. I will always remember you and Winslow in my prayers, trusting God to give you His comfort. Warm regards, Carol.*

Cecily crumpled up the letter and tossed it across the table. She then walked over to the coffee pot and poured herself a cup of coffee. She sat back down at the table, and as she sipped her drink, she tried to think of a plan. The one she had devised before her son had died didn't matter anymore. He was gone, and now her grandchildren were gone, too.

The more she thought about it, the angrier she became. Finally, she decided if she couldn't have her son, or her grandchildren, there was something she could get back. Of course, Winslow would put his foot down about it, but she figured he'd never need to know. She'd just make the call once he was out of the house.

Chapter Ten

Though she had tried to come up with every excuse in the books, Magnus and Abby would not let Carol sit home alone while they attended Floyd and Nova's Christmas party.

"Trust me," Magnus said. "You do not want to hurt Floyd's feelings. He may be big, but he has an even bigger heart that's easily wounded. Next time he sees you he'll be sure to let you know how he felt about you not being there...and besides, his wife is the sweetest woman. I think you will really like her."

"Do we have to stay long? I know it's the weekend, but I like to keep the kids on a strict bedtime schedule."

"I promise we'll be home before bedtime. Floyd is dressing up like Santa Claus for the kids, so even if you don't have a good time, I'm certain the kids will."

"Okay, what should I wear?"

"Oh, something festive," Abby said." I have a couple of Christmas sweaters you can borrow."

"No, thank you. I've seen your Christmas sweaters, Mom." Carol laughed. "I think I have a green blouse that will be festive enough."

"Perfect, we leave in an hour...um...you may want to put a little makeup on and…um…maybe do something with your hair." Abby raised her eyebrows at her daughter's appearance. Carol had pulled her hair up into a ponytail earlier in the day. By the time she had helped clean the house, it had come loose, leaving strands of hair flying in every direction.

"What are you saying? That I'm a mess?" Carol grinned. "If I go like this, then everyone will leave me alone. I'm really not in a social or festive mood."

"I think it will do you some good to get out of the house and meet some people," Magnus said. "We have a lot of new people in town. Believe it or not Snowflake Falls is becoming quite the happening place."

"Oh, sure, if you like Karaoke and a highly competitive game of Bingo. I drove by the Catholic church the other day and saw the same *Saturday Night Bingo* sign that they've had since I was in grade school!"

"Hey, don't go bashing Bingo. I won a hundred dollars last year!" Magnus laughed.

"Wow! Maybe I should go then. I could use some extra money. I'm not sure how I'm going to buy gifts for the kids…" Once again, she had opened her mouth without thinking. She really didn't want them to know about her dire financial situation. "I should be fine, though. I just need to make some time to go shopping."

"Carol, you don't need to worry about all that. Your mother and I have already bought the children plenty of gifts. I promise, the kids are going to have their best Christmas ever!"

"Dad…please. You can't keep doing this."

"I can't buy my grandchildren a gift?"

"It won't just be a gift. You'll buy the whole store for them!"

"It's what grandparents do! Stop being so stubborn about it. I know you'll get a job soon. As a matter of fact, the hospital will be hiring soon."

"How do you know that?"

"I talked to Mike, and he said they were about to hire several more nurses. It may not be until after the new year, but until then, we're happy to help you out financially."

"I wish you hadn't said anything. I don't want Mike to feel like he's obligated to put in a good word for me just because I'm related to his wife."

"It wouldn't just be a good word, Carol. You are a good nurse."

"Thanks for the vote of confidence, but I've been away from nursing since Blake was born. I also worry about the schedule I would have at the hospital. I was hoping to avoid working on weekends."

"Regardless of what schedule you have, you have a lot of family here. We are all eager to help you. You just need to let us know what we can do."

Carol took a deep breath in and slowly blew it out. "I know...it's just hard sometimes."

"You make it harder than it needs to be."

Carol sighed again. She didn't want to have this conversation right now. "I suppose if you want me to go to this party, I had better go get ready."

"We need to leave in about twenty minutes," Abby said.

"I thought I had an hour," Carol said as she looked at her mother.

"Technically we could leave in an hour, but you know your father, he always likes to be early."

"Oh, great!" She pulled the rubber band out of her hair and ran her fingers through the thick strands as she made her way upstairs to her room. Though she had no problem with leaving on her yoga pants and sweatshirt, she looked in her closet for something a bit more presentable so that her parents wouldn't be embarrassed by her appearance. She pulled down a green, silky blouse and a pair of black slacks. Once she was dressed, she looked in the mirror and groaned. She didn't have time to wash her hair, so she pulled it back up into a ponytail, but this time she twisted it into a knot and secured it in place with some pins. She then applied a little makeup.

Thinking a little jewelry would be nice, she began to dig around inside her jewelry box and found a gold necklace that Paul had given to her for their first anniversary. On the end of the chain was a heart-shaped pendant. On the back Paul had engraved the words *Mine Forever.* The reminder was more than she could handle. She dropped the necklace back inside the box then slammed the lid shut. She looked up at her reflection in the mirror and saw the fresh tears forming in her eyes. "Stop crying," she whispered. "It doesn't help."

She made her way back downstairs and was surprised to find all three of her children dressed in matching green sweaters with an elf on the front. Just below the elf were the words, *I'm the Cutest Elf.* They were also all wearing green and red striped elf hats. Carol began to laugh as soon as she saw them.

"What do we have here? Are you guys lost? The North Pole is that way," she said as she pointed north.

"Mommy! We're elves!" Lizzie said as she twirled around the room.

"I see that! You all look very cute!"

"Nana bought these for us, and guess what else?" Blake said excitedly.

"I can't imagine," Carol said, shaking her head.

"There are lots of presents under Papa and Nana's bed."

"Hey! You weren't supposed to look under there!" Magnus said as he pulled Blake up into his arms. "You're a sneaky elf, that's what you are!"

Blake wrapped his arms around Magnus' neck and gave him a tight hug. "I love you, Papa."

"I love you, too, buddy," Magnus said with misty eyes. "I love all of you very much. Have I told you how happy I am that you're all here?"

"Yes," Lizzie said as she ran over to him and wrapped her arms around his legs. "You've told us a bazillion times." She giggled.

Magnus bent down and also scooped Lizzie up into his arms. "Really, I thought it was more like a gazillion times."

"Papa, you're so funny," Lizzie said as she kissed his cheek.

Zoe wasn't happy that she wasn't getting any attention. She toddled over to Magnus and held her arms up in the air. "Up, Papa!" She demanded.

"Okay, hold on tight you two!"

Both Lizzie and Blake grabbed hold of his neck and clung tightly all the while laughing as he managed to stoop down and pick up Zoe, too. His arms surrounded all three of them, and soon he was showered with hugs and kisses from all three.

Abby and Carol stood back and watched with huge smiles on their faces. "They're so happy here. I'm glad that they have a strong male figure to look up to. I just wish that Paul's parents would have wanted…"

"Oh, speaking of Paul's parents, I completely forgot to tell you that Cecily called."

"What? When?" Carol's eyes widened as she looked at her mother.

"It was yesterday. I'm so sorry that I forgot to tell you."

"What did she want?" Carol asked, knowing it probably wasn't good if it was Cecily calling.

"She didn't really say. She just wanted to talk to you. I gave her your new cell phone number, so I suspect she'll be calling you soon."

"Hopefully, she wants to come see the children," she whispered to her mother.

"That would be wonderful. Maybe I should invite them to come for Christmas?"

"You can try, but this isn't their favorite place in the world to travel to."

"Well, it should be. You just have to remind them that the scenery is beautiful here," she said as she pointed to Magnus, who was now sitting on the couch, but still had all three kids in his arms.

"It is pretty spectacular, isn't it?" She smiled.

"Yes, and we better be going before he gets them too wound up. Nova has a lot of breakables at her house, so we better give them the "don't touch anything" speech on the way over."

"They've heard that speech a time or two." She laughed. "We'll just need to keep our eye on Zoe." As she went to get her coat she said, "We're not staying very long anyway, right?" Carol glanced at her mother while she nodded her head to remind her that they had agreed to leave early.

"If that's the case, we better get going then." Abby walked over to Magnus and pulled Zoe up into her arms.

"Come on, kids let's get your coats on," Carol said. "I understand that Santa is going to be at the party. I bet he's going to be looking for some backup elves."

***

Nova Emerson was greeting another couple at the door when they arrived, so they waited on the porch. Carol was immediately impressed with the pretty, older woman. She was petite with silver hair that shined brightly as it captured the light from the porch. Her smile was just as bright.

"Natalie and Jonathon!" Nova said as she wrapped her arms around the young couple. "Just because you're married now is no excuse for you not dropping by to see me!"

"We see you every Sunday at church," Natalie said with a smile.

"Yes, but I miss our little chats with a cup of tea in hand."

"I'll stop by next week, but it will have to be herbal tea for me because…"

"Oh, my heavens!" Nova placed a hand on her heart, then whispered loudly, "Are you expecting?"

"Yes," Natalie whispered back with a big smile on her face.

"Oh, that's just wonderful!" Nova gathered the two in her arms again, hugging them both at the same time. "When is the big day?".

"August…the hottest time of the year," Jonathon answered. "It's okay, though. It will get me motivated to finally put those window air conditioners in."

"We'll be sure to have the shower at the beginning of the summer then. My ladies tea group will plan the whole thing. We'll have it right here in my backyard." She said with a soft, southern drawl.

"That would be lovely," Natalie said.

"Now, go on inside and be sure to tell Bubba the good news. He'll be tickled pink!"

As the couple made their way inside the house, Nova looked over at her other guests and clapped her hands with glee. "Magnus and Abby! I'm so glad you could come…and who are these cute elves you have with you?"

"These are our grandchildren, Blake, Lizzie and little Zoe," Magnus answered. "This is our oldest daughter, Carol. She just arrived a few weeks ago."

Nova's face instantly changed from joy to compassion. Her husband had already shared with her about his encounter with Carol and how the poor woman had lost her husband at such a young age. She reached out and took both of Carol's hands in hers. "I'm so pleased to make your acquaintance, Carol. I've heard so much about you. You made a huge impression on Bubba. He couldn't stop talking about you after he met you the other day."

"Yes, we met at the bakery," Carol said. "He made quite the impression on me, too."

"He does have a way of doing that." She giggled. "When I asked him where he had met you, he had to confess he was at the bakery which is off limits to him at least until after Christmas." She shook her head as she sighed. "I don't know what I'm going to do with that man and his love for Ginger's cinnamon rolls!"

"I think we've all got the same problem." Abby chuckled. "I suppose the only way to avoid them is for her to stop making them all together, and no one wants that."

"You're right about that," Nova said as she held the door open for them to enter. "Now, please come in. We have a house full, but that just means more love and laughter for us all to share."

"Thank you so much for inviting me and the kids," Carol said. "Is Floyd inside? I'd like to thank him, too."

Nova was much shorter than Carol, so she had to pull Carol's arm down so that she could whisper in her ear. "He'll be down in a few minutes. I suspect you'll hear him long before you see him." She giggled.

As if on cue, a loud "Ho! Ho! Ho!" bellowed down the stairway followed by a very tall, dark-skinned Santa with a fluffy, white beard. The children hadn't met Floyd yet and were in awe of the sight of him. "Wow!" Blake said. "Santa is as tall as Papa."

Lizzie broke free from Carol's hand and ran toward Floyd yelling, "Santa! Santa!" While Zoe, scared to death, wrapped her arms tighter around Magnus and hid her face in the side of his neck.

"Ho! Ho! Ho!" He bellowed as he bent down to scoop up Lizzie in his arms. "Who do we have here? Why, I think it's one of my elves. How did you escape the North Pole? Don't you have work to be doing, young lady?"

Lizzie began to giggle with glee. "It's me, Lizzie!"

"Lizzie? Are you on my nice list?"

Lizzie turned and looked at her mother. "Am I, Mommy?"

Carol made her way through the crowd of guests toward them. "I believe she has been very good, Santa." Carol smiled.

"Well, of course she has. Ho! Ho! Ho!" He then turned to Carol. "Does this little elf belong to you?"

"Yes, she does."

"Well, then I know for certain she has been a very good little girl."

Carol reached for Lizzie, saying. "Santa needs to visit with the other children. Let's go see if we can find your cousins. I know Adam is here somewhere." She looked around the room and suddenly froze in place as her eyes locked with Keith's.

"Lizzie!" A little boy came running in their direction.

"Kyle! Mommy, look, it's Kyle, my best friend." She tried to wiggle herself out of Carol's arms.

"Hold on. I'll put you down," Carol said as she lowered Lizzie to the floor.

"The two friends hugged and giggled, then hugged some more. Kyle then took Lizzie's hand and began to drag her across the room. "Come see my dad."

"Come on, Mommy!" Lizzie shouted as she ran off with Kyle.

She ran after her daughter and soon found herself face to face with Keith. "Hi," she said, realizing she was a little out of breath. She wasn't sure if it was chasing after Lizzie or if it had to do with being so close to him.

"Hi," he said with a smile.

"This is my daughter, Lizzie, by the way. I guess she and your little boy are friends at the preschool."

Keith bent down so he could look Lizzie in the eye. "Hi, Lizzie. You're the little girl I bumped into and knocked clear to the floor. I'm very sorry about that. Sometimes I don't look where I'm going."

"That's okay. It didn't hurt."

"Glad to hear it." He stood back up and gave Carol a quick up and down look, stopping back at her eyes, noticing how they had taken on the same color of green as her blouse. "You look nice."

She nervously ran a hand along one of the sleeves of her silky blouse. "This was as festive as I was willing to get."

"I don't really do festive, either. Lois managed to get me to at least where a little red." He grinned.

Carol loved the dark red sweater he was wearing and was glad to see it was free of any reindeer or snowmen. "I thought I would know more people here, but there are a lot of new faces I don't recognize."

"Yeah, I think that Floyd purposely invites newer people in town as a way of making them feel welcome."

"That's nice of him. I just met him the other day. He's an interesting man."

"Yeah, I haven't known him that long, but he seems to accept everyone as a friend."

Lizzie began to pull on Carol's hand. "Mommy, I want to go see Santa."

Just then Magnus and Abby walked over to them. Magnus reached out to shake Keith's hand. "Hey! It's good to see you again."

"It's good to see you, too," Keith said. He shook Magnus' hand then gave Abby a quick hug. "I see that Blake has already found Adam and Bobby. I can see them over there in the corner plotting who knows what," Keith said with a chuckle.

"Is Lois here?" Abby asked.

"Yes, she's in the kitchen helping Nova with the appetizers."

"Hey, Lizzie, why don't you and Kyle come with us to go see Santa," Magnus said as he took Lizzie's hand. "I'm sure Mommy and Mr. Bradley would like to visit for a while."

"Oh, no, you don't have to…" Carol began to panic at the thought of being left alone with Keith.

"Of course I don't have to, but I want to," Magnus said with a grin.

"I want some photos, okay?" Carol called out to her father as he was leaving.

"Don't worry, your mother will take lots of pictures."

After her parents left with the children, Carol looked up at Keith. "So…" She bit down on her lower lip trying to think of something coherent to say.

"I'm actually glad to see you here. I was going to call you on Monday."

"Keith, I told you…" She sighed loudly so that he would clearly hear her frustration with what she believed was him still trying to get her to go out with him.

"Sarah had her baby, so I'm officially without a nurse. If you're still interested in the position, it's yours. You can start next week if you're able."

"Do you have the authority to do that?"

"Do what? Hire you?"

"Yes. I don't think Ms. Price would approve."

"I took the liberty of calling your references. They couldn't say enough good things about you. I then chatted with Amanda and explained why you left so abruptly."

"What did you tell her?" She widened her eyes, worried he may have divulged too much.

"I told her that I had treated you badly earlier that same morning and that's why you were uncomfortable. I got off easy with a slap on the arm." He playfully rubbed his arm as if it still hurt.

"She must think I'm a mess!"

"No, she was actually quite impressed with you. She told me that if I wanted to, I could offer you the job. I guess the question is, do you want the job?"

"I do, but…" Her mind was racing with thoughts, most of which were worries.

"But what?" He finally spoke after patiently waiting for her answer.

"I'm never getting married again," she blurted out the words without thinking, then immediately regretted doing so. Her cheeks turned bright red as she looked around the room, hoping to find a quick escape from the awkward situation.

"Okay...well, if that's the case, you'll be happy to know that marriage is not one of the job requirements." He chuckled.

She shook her head, "Yes, of course, I know that, it's just…"

Seeing her discomfort, Keith decided to change the subject momentarily. "Say, would you like something to drink?"

"I would love a drink, thank you."

"I'll go see what they have." Just as he turned to leave, a voice called out from somewhere in the crowd. "Oh, my gosh! Carol, is that you?"

Carol looked around and saw Kitty Pickler, the pastor's wife at St. Timothy Lutheran Church, heading in their direction. Carol's entire face lit up as soon as she saw one of her old friends.

"You probably didn't realize it, Keith, but you're over here talking to Miss Corn Queen 2006."

"I heard something about that." He grinned. "Did you have to present a talent and strut around in a bikini?"

"Yes, and it was very cold outside in October." Carol laughed. "Kitty was Miss Corn Queen in 2005. She presented me with the crown the year I won."

"I'm curious to know what your talents were?" Keith asked with raised eyebrows.

"Mine was singing and dancing." Kitty answered first. "I did a fantastic tap number, and Carol…" She began to giggle. "Carol did an…um….informative routine on bandaging and administering CPR!" She was laughing now.

"I didn't know what else to do. I don't have many talents," Carol admitted a little embarrassed by her lack of entertaining abilities.

"Hey, bandaging isn't something just anyone can do." Keith tried to encourage her, though he was having a hard time trying not to laugh.

"Well, I guess it was good enough, because I won." Carol then turned to Kitty and hugged her tight. "I'm so happy to see you. You look fantastic. Marriage and motherhood suits you just fine."

Kitty brushed her long, sandy blonde hair off her shoulders. "Lucy Pearl is a mother's dream. She is the sweetest baby...well, toddler now. She's running all over the place."

"I can't wait to see her. Did you bring her tonight?"

"No, she has a little bug, so she's home with Erich. Hopefully, she'll be at church tomorrow. Will I see you two there?"

"Absolutely," Keith answered.

"I'm really looking forward to coming, too. I'm looking forward to finally meeting your husband. Mom and Dad really think highly of Rev. Pickler."

"I sort of like him, too." She smiled, but then began to frown as she eyed Carol's hair. "So...I like your hair, it's really pretty up like that, but..." Her entire face seemed to pucker inward as she further scrutinized Carol's hair.

As the town's beautician, Kitty was notorious for giving unsolicited advice on hair styles. She had no qualms about telling someone when they were due for a trim.

"I know, it's awful." Carol patted her hair to make sure all the strands were neatly tucked into the bun.

"No, it's not awful, but I can see that you need a few highlights."

"As soon as I have a steady income I do plan to come in to the beauty parlor and finally get a good cut. It's been a very long time. I know I'll get a lecture out of you for neglecting it so badly."

"Oh, honey, I won't lecture you, and I won't take a dime from you, either. You come in next week, okay?"

"I can't let you do that, Kitty. I want to..."

"Hush now! I can see you around ten o'clock on..."

Keith shook his head. "Nope, that's not gonna work."

"Why not?" Kitty asked.

"Yeah, why not?" Carol asked not liking how he had assumed he could speak for her.

"Because you'll be working at the clinic...isn't that right?" He wasn't going to leave the party without getting a firm commitment out of her.

Carol stood there for several moments, hoping she was about to make the right decision. The thought of finally having a paycheck won out. "Yes." She slowly nodded her head. "I will be working at the clinic."

Chapter Eleven

Carol was surprised that she was actually having a good time at the party. She was able to visit with old friends, and even made a few new ones. She also found herself laughing several times by Floyd's antics as Santa. He was so animated as each child sat on his lap. He would then listen with genuine interest to each of their requests.

Blake had asked for a new football, which Carol made a mental note of. She was incredibly thankful it wasn't something more expensive. A football she could do. However, she wasn't sure what to think when Floyd promised that Blake would not only have a new football, he would get a signed one by a real NFL star who would also take him to the park and toss it back and forth with him. Floyd had looked up at his son, Micah, when he made the promise, giving him a little nod to let Micah know he had a job for him to do. Micah smiled and gave his father a return nod to let him know he understood.

Zoe refused to sit on Santa's lap, especially once she saw Keith. She reached out her arms, wanting for him to hold her, which he was happy to do. When Carol tried to get Zoe to come back to her, she just shook her head and snuggled closer to Keith. "I'm so sorry. I guess she really likes you."

"I really like her, too," he said as he patted the little girl's back. "My kids never wanted to sit on Santa's lap at this age. Maybe next year Santa will be able to win her over."

"I suspect she'd just ask Santa for a box and a couple of bows anyway. She's easy, but Blake and Lizzie sometimes want more than they need."

"Tell me about it! I heard Bobby ask Santa for a horse!" He shook his head and grimaced. "If that wasn't bad enough, Floyd answered him by saying he would see what he could do about that!"

"Do you have a place to keep a horse?" Carol asked with a grin on her face.

"Nope...I barely have a place to park my car. You know what I think?"

"That Santa is purposefully trying to make our lives more difficult than they already are?" Carol said jokingly.

"Well, yeah there is that, but also that it was much easier when our children were babies and were happier with the bows and boxes instead of the actual gift inside. I think Zoe here may have figured out where the real fun is at, right Zoe?" He tickled her behind her ear, making her giggle.

Carol looked at the two and smiled. Tears began to sting her eyes as she watched how happy Zoe was. It had been so long since she had seen or heard giggles and laughter from her. Coming here had done wonders for all of her children, and now as she watched how wonderful Keith was with her daughter, she began to feel things she hadn't felt in a very long time. She was so caught up in her thoughts she didn't realize that Lizzie had skipped up to sit on Santa's lap.

"Oh, look, Lizzie is up next," Keith said.

Carol shook away her thoughts and looked over to where Santa was sitting. "I can't imagine what she's going to ask for. She'll probably want an entire farm!" Carol laughed as she moved a few steps closer so that she could hear what Lizzie was saying. However, when Lizzie sat on Santa's lap, she pulled down on his beard to get him to lean down. Once he did, she whispered something into his ear.

"Well, now, that's a doozie!" He laughed as he looked up at Carol. "Santa will do whatever he can to make sure you get exactly what you want for Christmas, Miss Lizzie."

Later, Carol tried in vain to get Floyd to tell her what Lizzie had asked for. "Sorry, my lips are sealed. I promised I would keep it a secret."

"Floyd, please!" She begged. "I'm going to try to go shopping next week, and she hasn't given me any clues what she wants. The football Blake asked for is an easy one."

"Now, don't you worry about that football. Micah has a storeroom of footballs that he's already signed."

"That's wonderful! How much do I owe him…."

"Now you stop that nonsense! There's no charge."

"Floyd…"

She stopped when Floyd held up a hand to her. "Now, tell me what you think Miss Zoe would like since she's too shy to come sit on my lap?"

"It's hard to say, but she's not very particular."

Floyd nodded his head. "I suspect that little one would like a nice soft, teddy bear to cuddle with."

"I'm sure she would." Carol smiled. "Thanks for the idea. I'll add that to my list."

"No, you won't. I'm taking care of that, too."

"Floyd! You can't buy all my gifts."

"These aren't from you. These are from Santa!" He grabbed hold of his belly and began to laugh.

"Thank you, but seriously, I don't want you buying…"

"This was all my sweet wife's doing. Her little tea club is buying gifts for all the children here this evening. It's a new tradition she and the other women are wanting to start. It brings her more joy than you can imagine. You wouldn't deprive my dear wife of joy now, would you?"

"No," Carol said with misty eyes. "I just can't believe people can be that kind and generous. I'm very grateful."

"Good…but…" He sighed as he shook his head. "I'm not sure what to do about your Lizzie's request. That girl is a real treasure. What she's asking for might be…not impossible…just a bit challenging."

"Will you at least give me a hint?"

"No, that would spoil the fun. I've still got two weeks left. I'm going to have to rely on God to help me out with this one, though. Miracles do still happen after all!"

"You certainly have my curiosity piqued. You will let me know if there's something I can do to help, won't you?"

"Nope, if I did that, you'd know what she was wishing for."

"I don't want her to be disappointed this Christmas. I'm afraid last year was disappointing for all of us. We didn't even get a tree."

"What? Why not?" He looked shocked by the notion of not having a tree.

"Well, their father had just died the month before. I just couldn't bring myself to…"

"I see." He held up his hand letting her know she didn't have to say anything more. "That gives me even more motivation to make sure she gets her wish. I can't promise I will, but I do promise that I'll give it all I've got."

"I'm sure you will, but it would be a whole lot easier if you just…."

He held up his hand again. "I gave her my word."

She sighed knowing she wasn't going to get anything out of him. "Okay, okay. I'll let it go. Thank you for caring about her wishes, though. You are a dear man. I'm so glad I came tonight. I didn't want to, but…"

"I know you didn't, but I'm sure glad you did. Now, I have to ask, I noticed you spending quite a bit of time with Dr. Keith. Are you and him becoming sweet on each other?"

"No...no...um...nothing like that. It's just I'm going to be working with him at the clinic."

"Are you a nurse?"

"Yes, though I haven't worked in a while."

"So...you'll be working in Dr. Keith's office?"

"Yes, his nurse just had a baby and plans to stay home."

"Hmm…" He slowly ran his fingers down his fake beard several times as he looked closely at Carol.

The way he was looking at her made her nervous. "Why are you staring at me like that?"

"No reason…no reason at all." He began to laugh.

Carol wanted to find out what Floyd thought was so funny, but Keith came up behind her and tapped her on the shoulder. "I have something I think belongs to you."

Carol turned around to find Keith holding a sleeping Zoe in his arms. Her head was nuzzled up close to his neck. "I don't mind keeping her, though. She really is such a sweetheart."

"I'll take her," Magnus said as he came up behind them. As he gently pulled Zoe into his arms, he said, "Your mother already has Blake and Lizzie's coat on. You'll find yours in the bedroom closest to the restroom."

"Thanks, Dad. I'll meet you all out in the car."

While Carol made her way to the room to find her coat, Floyd caught Keith by the arm and pulled him close to his side. He then whispered near his ear. "Now, listen close. Whatever you do, don't take no for an answer."

"Okay…" He laughed. "But I'm not sure I know what you're talking about."

"I'm talking about when you ask that pretty lady to go to dinner with you tomorrow after church. She'll hem and haw about it, I'm certain of that, but don't take no for an answer."

"Are you telling me I should ask Carol out on a date?"

"Yes, and you better get to it before she leaves...now git!"

"You know, Santa, I didn't realize you were a matchmaker, too."

"Well, I am. Especially, when I see two grown adults who are obviously interested in each other but won't do anything about it. Life is too short not to act on all those feelings the two of you are having for one another!"

"Well, for the record, I have asked her out, but she didn't seem interested."

"Oh, she's interested...just a little scared, that's all. Now, stop flapping your jaw and git in there!"

Keith couldn't help but laugh as he walked down the hallway to the bedroom where he found Carol sifting through the large pile of coats on top of the bed. "Hey, do you have a second?"

Carol jumped at his voice. "Oh, you scared me. I didn't realize you were there."

"Sorry, I saw you come in here. I just wanted to ask you something."

"I don't really have much time to talk, Keith. My parents are waiting for me in the car."

"This won't take long. I was just wondering if you would like to have dinner with me tomorrow. We could call it a celebration dinner."

"Celebrating what?"

"Your new job, of course."

"I don't know, Keith, and besides, you won't find much open on Sunday."

"There's this nice place up in the mountains. I know it's open because I recently called asking about their hours."

"Are you talking about the Smokey Moose?'

"Yeah, that's the one! I hear they have really good burgers."

"They do, my family used to go to the mountains for skiing every winter. We'd have dinner there on our way home. But...that place is almost two hours from here."

"I know. That would give us plenty of time to talk...you know, to get to know each other better."

"It sounds like you're asking me out on a date."

"It's been a while, but yes, I think that's what I'm doing."

"You are persistent, aren't you?"

"It's my middle name." He chuckled.

"Thank you for the invitation, but I don't..."

He remembered Floyd's advice and blurted out, "I'm not taking no for an answer."

Her eyebrows raised at that. "Well, sorry, but that's not for you to decide."

"Come on, Carol. It's just dinner."

"You said it was a date."

"Is there really a difference?"

"To me...yes. A date implies that you have an interest in me, where dinner is just two people eating food together."

"Okay, we'll just call it dinner...eating food together. Will you say yes to that?"

"Do you promise it's not a date?"

He answered by laughing.

"I'm serious, Keith. You and I are going to be working very closely together. I don't want things to get...awkward."

"I promise, things will never get awkward. We'll be too busy for that."

"I don't know…" She shook her head.

"Not that again! You do know that you're just too afraid to take a chance, don't you?"

"I'm not afraid, it's just there's so much you don't know about me."

"Exactly, that's why I want to...um...go eat food with you…" He tried not to smile. "Carol, I want to get to know you better."

"What about the children?"

"What about them?"

"I don't know what they would think about me going to dinner with you. Then there's all the people in town. Who knows what they'll think! I hate that so much about this place. You haven't lived here long enough to know how they make it their business to know your business. I wouldn't want to put you through that...or myself for that matter."

"Are you done, yet?"

"Done with what?"

"Making excuses."

She shook her head. "I…"

He didn't allow her to continue. He reached out his hands and cupped the sides of her face. She tried to look away, but he gently kept her head steady so that she had no choice but to look into his eyes. She was surprised by what she saw there and even more surprised when he whispered, "Carol, I can't stop thinking about you."

His mouth was so close to hers that she could feel the warmth of his breath on her face. She whispered back, "I'm not any fun to be around. You'll probably just regret going anywhere with me."

"I don't think so." He slowly shook his head. "Just say yes."

She nodded her head.

Keith's eyes lit up. "Is that a yes? You'll go on a date with me?" He asked excitedly.

"Yes, I'll have dinner with you," she corrected.

"Ho! Ho! Ho!" Floyd bellowed from the doorway of the bedroom. He then walked into the room and slapped Keith on the back. "Did I hear right? You and this pretty woman are going on a date?"

"No…it's just dinner." Keith smiled as he continued to stare at Carol. "So, I'll pick you up tomorrow afternoon around three."

"That should be fine." She then turned to look at Floyd. "Thank you again for inviting me to the party. I had a really good time."

"I'm as pleased as punch that you came. I trust that you will have a very Merry Christmas, and you tell your sweet Lizzie that things are working out just fine."

"Floyd," she said as she placed her hands on her hips. "I don't know what you're up to, but…"

"Floyd isn't up to anything…this is Santa you're talking to, remember? Ho! Ho! Ho!"

Not knowing what to say to that, she just shook her head as she put on her coat.

"The mountains, huh?" Floyd slapped Keith on the back again. "Smart thinking!"

"What exactly does that mean?" Carol asked suspiciously.

"I don't know about you, but when my Nova is cold she likes to snuggle by the fire."

"Well, on that note…" Carol laughed nervously, "I'll be on my way. Good night, Floyd." She then turned back to Keith and smiled. "I'll see you tomorrow."

Once she got out to the car, she purposely sat next to Lizzie. While the others were chatting about the evening, Carol leaned close to Lizzie and asked, "Sweetheart, what did you ask Santa for?"

"The best present ever!" She said happily.

"Oh, yeah, what would that be...the best present ever, that is?"

"I can't tell you, Mommy. It's a surprise."

"I know, but could I have just a little hint?"

"Mommy!" Lizzie scolded. "You have to wait until Christmas!"

Carol decided right there and then that she didn't like surprises. Especially ones being concocted by a four-year-old child and an overly zealous Santa Claus!

Chapter Twelve

It took a little while that evening to get the children in bed. They were all very excited and couldn't stop talking about the town's Santa and how he wasn't at all like the one in Chicago. Both Blake and Lizzie agreed that the Snowflake Falls Santa was so much better!

After tucking Lizzie and Zoe into bed, Carol kissed them goodnight then shut the door behind her. The girls had finally moved out of her room and were now sharing a room together. Both of her girls were very active sleepers, and she had the bruises to prove it! Since they had moved out of her room, she was getting so much more sleep.

She went back downstairs to get a glass of water and just as she was heading back up the stairs, her cell phone began to ring. She looked down and instantly recognized the area code from Chicago. She took a deep, calming breath then answered, "Hello."

"Carol, this is Cecily."

"Oh, hi, Cecily. I heard that you had called the other day. How are you and Winslow doing?"

"I didn't call for chit-chat, Carol."

"Okay, why did you call then?" She continued up the stairs and entered her bedroom being sure to shut the door behind her. She already suspected that this was not going to be a friendly phone call and didn't want her parents to overhear her conversation.

"Did you realize that the ring that Paul gave you belonged to my mother?"

"Yes, I knew that. It's a beautiful ring." She looked down at it and sighed. She hadn't been able to bring herself to take it off yet.

"I never wanted him to give it to you, but he insisted."

"Cecily, it's late here. I was on my way to bed." She was tired and in no mood for her negativity.

"Okay, so I'll get right to the point. I want the ring back."

"You want the ring back?" Carol wasn't sure she had heard correctly.

"Yes, and I want it as soon as possible."

"It's highly unusual to ask for a wedding ring back, Cecily. I understand that the ring is special to you, but it might be something Blake will want to give to his bride on his wedding day."

"Carol, that ring is worth twenty-thousand dollars! I'm sure you can understand why I want it back. With your financial situation, I don't want you tempted to sell it!"

"I would never sell it." She was horribly insulted by the accusation.

"You know, we loaned Paul quite a bit of money. We'll never get that back now that he's…" She couldn't bring herself to say the word.

"I'm sorry. I didn't realize that he had borrowed money from you." She closed her eyes and rubbed her temples, not wanting to hear that Paul had yet another secret he had kept from her.

"Well, he wanted you and the kids to have that nice house. Who do you think provided the down payment for it? And of course, the tuition to that private preschool was more than Paul could afford. You did know that we paid for Blake to go there, didn't you?"

Carol didn't know that, but she didn't want to admit that to Cecily. "I am very appreciative of everything you did for us, but this is the ring that Paul gave to me on our wedding day. It now belongs to me. I'm keeping it, Cecily."

"I don't think so. I will be getting that ring back…even if I have to hire a lawyer."

"You would go to court over this?"

"If it has to come to that, absolutely!"

"Cecily…" She sighed, unable to say anything else, knowing she wouldn't be heard anyway.

"It would make it easier for everyone if you just sent the ring back to me. Make sure I have to sign for it, and take out insurance when you mail it. Like I said, it's worth quite a bit."

"I'm not sending you the ring. I will make sure that it's well cared for, and like I said, I will give Blake or the girls the option to use it one day if they so choose."

"Carol! You will send me that ring!"

Carol hung up, even though she could still hear Cecily yelling in the background. Her good mood after the party was all but gone now as she miserably sat down on the edge of her bed staring down at the ring, remembering when Paul had slipped it on her finger during their wedding ceremony. She remembered how her hand had trembled as he had placed it on her finger. "Paul," she had whispered. "It's beautiful."

He hadn't let her see it before the wedding. He wanted it to be a surprise. His face had lit up with pride when he saw her reaction to it. He later had shared that it had once belonged to his grandmother. Since he was her only grandson, she had wanted him to have it and had made it official by including it in her will.

Every time Carol looked at it during their honeymoon she would insist that it was too much. Paul would hush her by saying she was more than worth it, and that she deserved only the best. They had been so in love on that day. It was hard to believe that all their hopes and dreams had come down to, *I don't love you anymore*. She was haunted by his last words to her. How had they come to that?

As she stared down at her wedding ring, she knew it was time. With a heavy sigh she willed herself not to cry as she slowly began to twist the ring off her finger. It always was just a little too big for her, so it slipped off easily. She held it in her hand for several minutes more, then stood up and placed it inside the jewelry box on her dresser.

She then slipped into bed and cried herself to sleep.

Chapter Thirteen

Carol looked at herself in the mirror and smiled. The reflection was of the woman she had once known, someone she had forgotten even existed. Her long, silky brown hair fell softly around her shoulders. She had only used a little makeup, but it had made a huge difference in her appearance, especially by erasing some of the dark circles under her eyes from her lack of sleep the night before. She wasn't sure what to wear, but decided to go more casual with a cable knit sweater and jeans, knowing the restaurant wasn't the least bit fancy.

She jumped when the doorbell rang. She gave herself one more look in the mirror, running her fingers through the bouncy curls. She breathed in deeply, then grabbed her purse and coat and made her way down the stairs.

Abby was heading toward the door, but Carol stopped her. "I'll get it, Mom."

"You look just lovely," Abby whispered.

"Mom," Carol whispered back. "Should I be doing this?"

"Yes, you should be. You're going to have a wonderful time. Now go open the door before he freezes to death out there."

She took one last calming breath, nervously ran her fingers through her hair once more, then finally opened the door. Just as soon as she laid eyes on him, it felt as if her heart had literally stopped beating. He was also wearing jeans with a chocolate colored sweater that matched the color of his eyes perfectly. From where she stood she could smell his aftershave, a pine, woodsy scent that seemed appropriate for their drive up to the mountains.

She started to smile, but it quickly faded when she noticed what he was carrying in his hands.

"These are for you," Keith said as he handed her a bouquet of roses.

She stood in the doorway and looked at the flowers as if he was offering her poison. She began to shake her head. "No, I can't take those." She took several steps back into the house. She was about to close the door in his face, but as he had done before, he held out his hand to keep the door from shutting.

"Are you okay?" He asked, concerned by the look on her face.

"This isn't a date. I thought I made that clear!"

Abby and Magnus heard Carol at the door and immediately became worried by the tone of her voice. Abby rushed to the door and saw Keith standing there with a baffled look on his face, still holding the bouquet in his hand.

"Those are simply beautiful!" Abby said. "Here let me take those." She reached out and took the bouquet out of his hand. "I'll go put these in a vase for you, sweetheart."

Carol shook her head, but it seemed as if her vocal cords were paralyzed. She felt the panic begin to rise inside of her. She desperately needed to escape before she lost control of her emotions. "I...I'm not feeling very well. I don't think I should…" She turned and ran up the stairs to her bedroom leaving Keith at the door in a bit of daze and unsure of what he should do.

"I'm so sorry, Keith," Abby said as she opened the door wider. "Please, come in."

"Is she okay?" He asked as he stepped inside the house.

"Yes, she's just having a hard time right now." Abby was aware that Carol was having panic attacks. She didn't know exactly how to help her with them, only that they should keep things as calm as possible for Carol until the panic eased up.

"I thought she would like the flowers. I'm sorry if I've upset her."

"It was a lovely gesture. Please, don't feel bad about it. It's hard to know what might set her off these days."

"I completely understand." He nodded his head.

"I'll go talk to her. Why don't you go visit with Magnus. I'll try to get her to come back down."

"If you don't mind, I'd like to go talk to her."

"I don't know…" Abby shook her head.

"I understand what she's going through. I think I can help."

"Okay," Abby said. "Her room is upstairs. It's the second door on the left."

Keith quietly walked up the stairs. The door to Carol's room wasn't shut all the way, so he pushed it open and entered as quietly as he could. "Carol," he spoke softly, not wanting to alarm her.

She abruptly raised her head and turned it toward him. "Please, just leave me alone."

"Yeah, I guess I could do that...but I'm not going to," he said as he walked toward the bed where she was sitting.

"Keith, please," she begged. "I'm not ready. I won't ever be ready. I can't do this again."

He sat down next to her and put his arm around her shoulders then pulled her close to his side. "I have a strong shoulder."

She sighed as she leaned her head against his shoulder. "I'm sorry," she said as she wiped the tears from her cheeks. "I told you that I wasn't any fun to be around right now."

"What are you talking about? This is fun." He chuckled. When he heard her soft laughter, he was hopeful that she was beginning to calm down. "I know it's hard, but I promise it does get a little easier." He could feel her shaking her head, so he added, "I promise, Carol. It won't always feel this way."

"It's not what people think."

"What do you mean?"

"I don't want to talk about it. I just think it's best if you leave. I'm not worth all this trouble I keep putting you through."

"I happen to think you are worth it. I also think that you are a very strong woman."

"Obviously, I'm not very strong right now." She wiped again at the tears she wasn't yet able to control.

"Tears don't make you weak. I remember the first few months after Kim had died. I couldn't function at all. I couldn't even cry. You're lucky that you still can."

"Can I ask you a personal question?"

"You can ask me anything."

"How did your wife die?"

"She died of a brain aneurysm. She wasn't feeling well that morning, but I didn't think anything of it. Later that afternoon, one of our neighbors called me at work and told me I should come home because she had seen an ambulance in the driveway. Lois was away visiting her other daughter, so I knew it wasn't her. My fear was something had happened to one of the boys. When I ran inside the house I was shocked to find Kim lying on the kitchen floor surrounded by EMTs. Our oldest, Bobby, was only three, but he had managed to call 911. I just stood there dazed and confused. It was as if all my medical training went out the door. I literally had no idea what to do."

"That must have been awful for you," she said with empathy.

"It was the worst day of my life."

"I'm so sorry," she whispered.

"None of it made sense to me then or now."

"Did you love your wife?"

His eyes widened in surprise by that question. He wasn't sure why she would ask that, but he still answered it. "Yes, of course. We loved each other very much. Can I ask you a question now?"

"Um...I guess, but I'm not really ready to talk about Paul."

"I understand, but I'm curious about something. Do you not like flowers?"

She shook her head. "No, I love flowers."

"Just not roses?"

"I love roses. It was sweet of you to bring them. It's just Paul used to send flowers every week, before..."

"I see...you miss getting flowers from him."

"No," she said as she shook her head. "It's not that at all."

"Then what is it, Carol?"

"It's just that flowers remind me…" She couldn't say the rest out loud. It was too painful. Paul had always sent her weekly flowers…but then they stopped just as his love had stopped. In her mind, flowers were a reminder to her that her husband had stopped loving her.

"Come on, talk to me. I don't ever want to do anything to hurt you. I need to know why the flowers affected you that way."

"I can't." She shook her head.

"Okay...so, let me ask you this. Do you think you can still have dinner with me?"

"Do you still want to? I wouldn't blame you one bit if you didn't."

"Oh, I definitely still want to. Besides, I'm starving."

"Okay, well, let me go see if I can repair the damage I've caused to my face."

He reached down and lifted her chin so that he could look into her eyes. "I don't see any damage. You are very beautiful, Carol. The very second that I saw you at the door, my heart began to race."

"Mine did, too." She admitted shyly.

"Yeah?"

"Just a little." She smiled.

"There's that smile I love to see."

"I'm sorry. I know I can be difficult. I just can't seem to pull out of this."

"You will. Come on…" He stood up and reached for her hand. "We better get going. I want to get up there before it gets dark."

When he took her hand, he pulled a little too hard causing her to fall into his arms. He instantly wrapped them around her. "Now I've got you just where I want you." He laughed.

Just then the door flew open and Blake and Lizzie came running into the room screaming at each other. "It's mine! Mama, tell him he can't have it!" Lizzie shouted.

"Papa gave it to me!" Blake responded loudly.

Carol began to laugh. "Are you sure about this? I come with a lot of baggage."

"You think you've got baggage? Sweetheart, you ain't seen nothing yet! I bet my two boys are giving their grandmother a run for her money right now."

"Blake, Lizzie, you're being very rude in front of our guest. What are you two fighting about?"

"Papa said I could have the fast sled, but now Lizzie wants it."

"How about you share the sled."

"Do we have to?" Lizzie pouted.

"No, you don't have to. You could just stay home and not go sledding at all."

"We'll share," Blake said. He then quickly left, leaving Lizzie standing there, staring up at them.

"Lizzie, I think I hear Papa calling for you. He's probably ready to go sledding."

"Do you like my mommy?" Lizzie asked Keith, giving him a curious look.

"Yes, I do. Is that okay?" Keith asked.

"Yes, it's okay." Her smile was huge as she turned to leave.

"Four down, one to go," Keith said with a grin.

"What are you talking about?"

"Well, one of your concerns was that you weren't sure what the kids would think about us. We know Zoe is okay with me, now Lizzie is, too. I just need to get Blake's approval."

"You're forgetting that I need the approval of Bobby and Kyle."

"Who do you think practically pushed me out the door when they heard I was coming over here to see you."

"Your boys hardly even know me."

"Yeah, but you're Blake and Lizzie's mother and they both love Blake and Lizzie, so that makes you okay in their books." He chuckled.

"We have great kids, don't we?" Carol said as she pulled away from him.

"Yeah, we do, but they've been through a lot."

"I know. No child should have to lose a parent at such a young age," Carol said.

"No, they shouldn't, but just like us, they're going to be okay."

"Thank you," she said as she reached for his hand.

"For what?"

"For putting up with all my emotional outbursts."

"It's perfectly normal to feel the way that you do."

"I know, but I want...no I need to get over this."

"You just take it one day at a time, Carol. Don't look too far forward and only look back if you're feeling lost."

"One day at a time. I think I can do that."

"So, for today we have…dinner." He said with a smile as he led her out the door.

"Yes, dinner," she said, knowing full well this was about to be far more than just dinner.

Chapter Fourteen

Magnus managed to fit Blake, Lizzie and Zoe all on his lap as they got ready to slide down the hill. "Okay, Nana, give us a push...but not too hard," he said.

"No, push us hard!" Lizzie shouted with glee. "I want to go fast!"

"Okay, but hold on tight to Papa," Abby instructed. She then began to count, "One…two…three!" Abby gave them a push that sent them spiraling down the hill in the large inner tube that Magnus had recently purchased. This was the one that Blake and Lizzie were arguing about because it was considered the fast sled, which they were all just now finding out was indeed very fast.

They screamed with delight as they made their way down the steep hill. Once at the bottom, they toppled to one side, sending all four of them flying. Everyone was laughing except for Zoe who began to wail.

Abby could hear Zoe crying from the top of the hill, so she ran down to where they were at, falling a few times herself on the slippery slope. "Is everyone okay?"

"We're all fine," Magnus said, trying to wipe the snow off of Zoe's face. "Apparently, Zo-zo doesn't like snow in her face."

"Come on, Zoe. Let's get you some hot chocolate and warm you up," Abby said as she gathered the crying child in her arms.

"I want some, too," Lizzie said as she followed close behind them.

"Do you think we should go down one more time?" Magnus asked Blake. "It's already starting to get dark, so we'll need to pack up soon."

"Yeah! Let's do it!"

"Okay, we'll do one more run."

On the way back up the hill, Blake asked, "Papa, when is Mommy coming home?"

"Well, I'm not really sure. She's on a date...well, dinner, as she calls it."

"Does Mr. Bradley like Mommy?"

"It kind of looks that way...but then again, who wouldn't like your mother. She's smart, she's kind...I'd say that you are very blessed to have her as your mother, don't you think?"

"Oh, yeah! I love Mommy, but you know what?"

"What?" Magnus asked as he looked down at his grandson.

"Daddy didn't love her."

Magnus stopped walking and bent down in the snow so he could look directly into Blake's eyes. "Why would you say something like that? Your father loved your mother very much."

"No, he didn't. I heard him tell her that he didn't love her anymore and that he was leaving."

"When did you hear him say that?"

"On the night he didn't come home. He was mad at Mommy and told her he was leaving for good. He was really, really loud, and she was crying."

"You heard your father yelling?"

"Yeah, he didn't want to get Zoe's medicine. He was mad at Mommy for making him go get it. I was worried because I thought that maybe he didn't love me, too."

"Oh, buddy, I know that your father loved all of you very much. You just misunderstood what he said."

"Nope," Blake said adamantly as he shook his head. "I heard him say it! He slammed the door so hard a picture fell off the wall! He wanted a d...d...vorze."

"Papa!" Abby called down the hill. "Are you two coming?"

"Yeah, we're coming!" He grabbed hold of Blake's hand. "I wouldn't worry about all this. Sometimes adults just say things they don't mean to say."

"Why?"

"I don't know, we just do."

"Did you ever tell Nana that you didn't love her?"

"No, I would never…" He looked down at Blake again. "Have you talked to your mother about this?"

"No, I don't want her to cry. She cries a lot. But, since I'm the oldest, I think I should help her so she won't cry anymore."

"You're a good boy." Magnus patted his grandson's shoulder. "I tell you what, Nana and I will talk to your mother and try to figure this out, okay?"

"Okay."

"I don't want you to worry about this anymore. Do you think you can do that?"

"I'll try."

"Good. What do you say we have some of Nana's hot chocolate before we go down the hill again."

"Yeah!" He then ran the rest of the way up the hill.

When they joined the others, Abby could tell something was wrong by the look on Magnus' face. "Here, Blake, come get a cup of hot chocolate while I talk to Papa." She handed a cup to Blake, then grabbed hold of Magnus' hand and pulled him out of hearing range. "What's wrong? What were you talking to Blake about?"

"Abby, something is terribly wrong. I think Paul and Carol were having marital problems."

"She never said anything to me about it. As far as I knew, everything was just fine."

"Yeah, well, Blake just told me that they were going to get a divorce."

"What? No!" She shook her head. "She would have definitely talked to me about that. No, I'm sure they were just fine."

"I don't know. I can't imagine that Blake would make this up. He was pretty certain that he had heard Paul tell Carol that he didn't love her anymore and that he was leaving. He's now worrying that his father didn't love him, too."

"Oh, no. Poor baby. You told him that wasn't true, didn't you?"

"Of course, but it sounds like Paul and Carol had a terrible fight on the night he died. I can't imagine they would fight in front of the children, but Blake was very clear about what he heard."

"Do you think we should talk to Carol about it?"

"Yeah, I think we should. She needs to know that her son is worrying about all this. He thinks he needs to fix it so that his mother won't cry anymore."

"Oh, dear. He's way too young to be thinking he should fix adult problems."

"I know. Let's talk about this later with Carol. We can chat tonight when the kids go to bed."

"Okay." She inhaled deeply, then forced a smile on her face as she walked back over to where the children were finishing up their drinks. "Who's ready to go home?"

Lizzie and Zoe were both wet and cold, so they nodded their heads, but Blake ran toward his grandfather. "Just one more time down the hill! Please, Papa!"

"Yeah, come on, buddy." He turned to look at Abby. He could tell that she was still stewing over what he had just told her. "Nana, come give us a push."

She walked over and leaned her arms down to grab hold of the tube. Magnus looked up at her and patted her hand. "It's going to be okay."

"I hope so," she said quietly.

"What's going to be okay?" Blake asked.

"We are! Come on, give us a good push, Nana! We want to fly down this hill!"

Chapter Fifteen

"I've got to tell you, Keith, this is a really nice car., but…"
Her hand trailed across the soft leather seat. "I just don't think it's
very practical for driving up in the mountains during the winter.
The roads can get really slick up here."

"This car can handle anything," he boasted. "We'll be fine.
Besides, it's a beautiful day, there's not a cloud in the sky, the sun
is shining, and I've got the Harvest Fest Corn Queen by my side."
He glanced over at her and grinned.

"That was a long time ago. I only entered that contest to
get the attention of a guy I liked at the time."

"Oh, yeah? Who was that?

"His name was Bobby LaFoe." She began to laugh. "Oh,
my gosh! I haven't thought about him in years. My father
couldn't stand him and was mortified that I was head over heels
in love with a hoodlum, as he had called him."

"A hoodlum, huh?" He chuckled. "How old were you?"

"Sixteen."

"How old was he?"

"He was twenty."

"Oh, I see." He nodded his head. "I understand why your
father would be upset by that."

"My father used to be a teacher at the middle school and
had Bobby as a student. He told me that Bobby spent more time
in the principal's office than he did in class."

"Why did you like him?"

"He was cute!" She laughed. "I think I must have been
going through a rebellious stage or something. I knew my parents
didn't like him. I guess that made him more appealing to me."

"Did you ever go out with him?"

"I tried to. My plan was to sneak out of my bedroom
window which was on the second floor. I jumped off the roof and
broke my ankle. I was grounded for several months after that."

"Did Bobby still try to see you after all that?"

"No...but that was only because my father went to his apartment and told him that if he ever came near me, he would have him arrested. Thankfully, I'm able to laugh about it now, but at the time I felt like my whole world was ending."

"I take it that your father was a little protective."

"Not just a little," she said, shaking her head as she remembered how her father had always watched over her with an eagle's eye. "I understand it now, but at the time, it drove me nuts."

"Whatever happened to Bobby?"

"He ended up in jail for petty theft or something like that. Bobby LaFoe was a bad mistake in my life. He was the reason, however, that I decided I didn't want to stay in Snowflake Falls. I didn't want to live my life always having my father, and the people in this community, watching every move I made. The talk around town was never ending after I jumped off our roof. For a while, people had me pegged as the 'bad girl' in town for liking someone with such a sordid reputation."

"Yeah, small town gossip can get pretty bad at times."

"The rumor was that we were running off to elope." She shook her head and laughed.

"I think you were pretty lucky to have a father like Magnus."

"I realize that now that I have children of my own. My father was protecting me from what could have potentially been a terrible disaster."

"Well, I'm glad it all worked out for the better."

"Me, too…" She turned her head to look at him. "So, how about you? Any disasters you care to talk about?"

"No, not really. I pretty much knew Kim my entire life. We were friends since kindergarten. We started dating our sophomore year of high school. Neither of us had dated anyone else."

"That's very sweet." She smiled at him, thinking she would have probably liked him in high school, too.

"We got married right after college, and then she worked to put me through medical school. I'll always be grateful for the sacrifices she made for me."

Carol noticed that his eyes had turned glassy. "I'm sorry, Keith. We can talk about something else."

"No, it's good to talk about it." He assured her with a smile. "Tell me about your husband. How did you two meet?"

"Paul was my dentist."

"Really?" He looked over at her with raised eyebrows.

"Yes, in college I needed my wisdom teeth extracted. I made an appointment, and he was the one who had an opening that fit my schedule. We sort of hit it off from the moment he numbed my mouth." She chuckled softly at the memory of their first meeting. She realized, though, that the more she allowed herself to think about it, the more it seemed like it had all just been a dream. She sighed as she turned her head to look out the window.

Keith could tell that she was lost in thought. Her face had turned solemn as she peered out the window. He was afraid she was going to close up on him, so he thought he should try to move the conversation away from her husband. "So you moved to Chicago right out of high school?"

"That's right. I hit the road and never looked back." She shifted in her seat so that her body was turned more toward his. "As a matter-of-fact, I told myself I would never come back… well, for a visit every now and then, but I didn't want to live any where near Snowflake Falls."

"How did your parents feel about that?"

"They hated it, of course. I wanted to travel and see the world, which I did on most of my breaks. It was wonderful! I had the time of my life...then I met Paul…and well…life happened and now here I am, back in Snowflake Falls whether I wanted to be here or not."

"Yes, here you are." He glanced over at her again. "I'm really glad you agreed to have dinner with me."

"I'm glad that I did, too, but I feel like I need to remind you that it *was* a beautiful day when we left. I don't think that you've noticed those dark clouds in the horizon."

Keith had been so distracted by her that he hadn't noticed what was going on outside. "Really?" He cocked his head so he could see the sky better through the windshield. "I don't remember hearing about a storm headed in this area."

"I didn't listen to the weather this morning. Did you?"

"On Sunday? Are you kidding?" He chuckled. "There's no time for that. Getting two squirmy boys ready for church keeps me and Lois pretty busy. I don't know what I would do without her."

"I got a chance to meet her at the party. She's very sweet."

"Yes, she is. She didn't have to stay with us after Kim died, but she chose to, which in my opinion, makes her an exceptional woman."

"My parents wanted me to move in with them right after Paul died, but I wanted to prove I could make it on my own. I obviously wasn't able to, though." She sighed again and turned her body so that she was facing forward.

He reached over and touched her arm, causing her to look over at him again. "You probably did better than you thought you did. Sometimes we're our worst critics."

"I don't know, Keith." She shook her head. "I didn't have any help. Raising three young children alone was beginning to take a toll on me."

"What about Paul's parents. Where do they live?"

"They were just ten minutes from our home, but I rarely saw them."

"Why?" He seemed perplexed by that.

"My mother-in-law didn't particularly care for me."

"Are you serious? Who in their right mind wouldn't like you?"

"She wanted someone better for her son. I was from a small town. I didn't have all the social graces she was hoping for in a daughter-in-law. Obviously, my Corn Queen crown didn't impress her very much," she said with a smirk.

"Well, she was wrong to think that way."

"I don't know." She shook her head again. "Cecily and her husband, Winslow, are extremely wealthy people. They are part of a world that was so foreign to me. I knew I didn't fit in, but I wanted to so badly. The more I tried, though, the more Cecily would find fault in me. Most of my marriage was spent with her nit-picking about what I should or shouldn't be doing. Then after Paul died, the nitpicking became…I don't know…more cruel I guess."

"How so?"

"Well, for one, she blamed me for Paul's death."

"Blamed you?" He was appalled by the accusation. "Carol, his death was not your fault."

"I married him. If I hadn't have, he would still be alive."

"She told you that?" He shook his head angrily.

"Yes, she did. She also said had I been a better mother and had gone out earlier in the day to get Zoe's medicine, Paul would still be alive."

"That's crazy!" He said loudly. "I can't believe she would say something like that to you." He looked at her with compassion in his eyes. "I'm sorry you had to go through all that."

"No, I'm sorry. I shouldn't have brought it up." She looked out the window and could see the glistening of fresh tears in her reflection.

"Don't be sorry. You can talk to me about anything. I've been through all this, so I will always understand whatever it is you're going through."

"I don't think so, Keith. Our stories are not the same."

"Of course, they are. You and I both lost someone very special to us at a relatively young age. It's a horrible thing to go through. I feel like we can help each other, you just have to be willing to open up more about it. Just talk to me, Carol."

"You want me to talk to you about it?" She abruptly turned her head toward him, allowing him to see the deep sadness etched across her face. "I guarantee if I talk to you about all this, you'll turn this car around and hightail it back to Snowflake Falls!"

"Why would I do that?" He shook his head, not understanding why she would say something like that.

"Because...I'm a failure! I'm not someone that a person as wonderful as you should be with!" She didn't mean to shout it like that, but she had bottled it up inside for so long she couldn't stop it from spewing forth.

He noticed that the restaurant was just up ahead. He pulled into the parking lot, but he had no intention of getting out of the car just yet. Instead, parked the car, then turned toward her and said, "Talk to me."

"I want to, Keith. I really do. I'm just so scared."

"I promise there is nothing you can say…"

"Yes, there is...it's not what people think. I'm not mourning the loss of my husband!" She couldn't believe she had finally said it out loud. She lowered her head, not wanting to see his reaction.

He wasn't going to allow that, though. He reached out and placed his hand under her chin, lifting her head so he could look into her eyes. "Carol, just talk to me."

"I haven't told anyone, not even my parents...but I'm tired of everyone assuming I'm in deep mourning when I know that I'm not. You see…Paul and I…well, we weren't doing very well. We had grown apart. I don't exactly know why…he was too busy, I was too tired. It was a number of things. Things that could have been worked out, but…Paul was about to…" The panic began to rise. She breathed in and out several times to try to calm herself down, but no matter how hard she tried, she knew that she was about to come undone.

Keith saw her struggling, so he pulled her into his arms and held her close. "What was Paul about to do?"

She slowly breathed in an out, trying to calm herself. Finally, with her head pressed against Keith's chest, she closed her eyes and opened her heart to him. "Paul wanted a divorce," she began. "On the night that he went out into the storm to get the medicine for Zoe, he told me that he didn't love me anymore and that he was leaving me. He told me this right in front of the children." After the confession, she began to sob.

Keith didn't know what to say. He just held her and let her cry until her body was almost limp in his arms. "I'm so sorry, Carol. This has obviously been a huge burden for you to carry, hasn't it?"

She nodded her head. "I wasn't good enough for him. He always let me know it in subtle ways. I didn't dress right. I didn't fix my hair the right way. I didn't clean the house good enough. I wasn't taking care of the kids properly. The list of how I had failed him was quite long. I admit, after the children came, I had let myself go because I was just so exhausted. Our house was so big…it was just too much for me. I didn't want to live there, but he was the one who had insisted on the affluent neighborhood where keeping up with the Jones' was important to the people who lived there. At least, it certainly mattered to my husband. The lawn had to look a certain way, the furniture had to be the best. You always had to be prepared in case someone came over. You weren't allowed to show your messes. You had to keep up the appearance that everything was perfect. I just couldn't do all that and take care of the children at the same time."

"He didn't help you?"

"No, not really." She shook her head. "He worked long hours, so he was always tired when he got home from work. After the children came, he basically stopped coming home. I mean he did, but mentally and emotionally he wasn't there anymore."

"Work stress can do that to a person."

"He was definitely stressed, and I was exhausted. I love my children with all my heart, but my marriage was falling apart at the seams. I kept telling myself that once the children were older it would get better. Because of that, I never told anyone what was happening between Paul and I. Everyone assumed we were doing fine, but we weren't. I do know this, though, I would have fought for our marriage to the bitter end. I would have done whatever it took to keep us together. I made promises to him on our wedding day…for better or for worse. I knew things were bad, but I always fully believed if we just made an effort we could work it out…I just never got the chance to prove that to him. I'll never know what might have happened. All I know is that the last thing he said to me was that he didn't love me anymore. I know I should have told someone, my parents at least, but I was...embarrassed. They always had such high expectations of me, and I let them down. That's why I can't ever get married again. I'm just no good at it!"

Keith had listened carefully to everything she had shared, even to the end when she stated she couldn't ever get married again. A part of him wondered if she really meant that. He knew that he could be wasting his time getting to know this woman who had no intention of developing a meaningful relationship with him, one that could lead to marriage. Right now, though, all he wanted to do was keep holding her.

"So...are you ready to turn the car around?" She leaned back and looked up at him.

"Sorry, you're not getting rid of me that easy."

"Keith, I'm a disaster. You don't want to be with someone like me."

"Hey, let me be the judge of that." He brushed a strand of hair away from her face. "I know this example is cliche, but you know the whole analogy of the glass half empty or half full?"

"Yes, but I don't see…"

"Let me finish. You are viewing all that happened from the glass half empty way of looking at things. You see yourself as a failure, but it was Paul who talked about leaving you. You're the one who said, 'I would have fought to the bitter end to save my marriage.'"

"Yes, but I could have done more, I could have…"

"Carol, everyone can do more to work on their marriages. It sounds like he could have done more to help you around the house and with the kids. Let me ask you this, if he had come home that evening, what were you planning to do?"

"Um…" she paused so she could take a moment to remember. "I had already fed the children and had put them to bed. I then prepared dinner for him. I had waited so that I could eat with him. I was hoping we could talk. I wanted to find out what was wrong."

"Exactly, you weren't going to just accept that he might go pack his bags and stay in a hotel. You were going to try to work it out. The problem is, you never got to do that. You never got to prove to him what a strong and tenacious woman you are. You never got to show him what fighting for a marriage looks like. I suspect you're really angry at him for that."

"Maybe, I don't know. I just keep reliving that moment over and over when he looked me in the eye and told me he didn't love me anymore. It's been a nightmare for me that those were his last words."

"I know what you mean. I went through my own demons after Kim died. You know what my last words to my wife were?"

"What?"

"I was in hurry, much like I was on the day when I met you. You know first hand what a jerk I can be when I'm rushed like that."

"Well, yeah, you were a little jerky." She grinned.

"Kim stayed home with the kids since they weren't in school yet, but she would always get up at the same time that I did to make me breakfast. It had become our special time together. It was really nice."

He stopped for a moment to remember how wonderful that time together had been. He breathed in and out a few times, then continued. "On that particular day, she was overly tired and didn't get up until it was too late to make breakfast. Because I knew she always did make breakfast for me, I didn't bother to make anything even after I realized she wasn't getting up. By the time she finally walked into the kitchen, I was already heading out the door. She was saying something about how she wasn't feeling very well, but I didn't care. I just looked at her and very sarcastically said to her, "Thanks for breakfast." Then I left. I always kissed my wife goodbye, but on that day I didn't because I was angry with her. Once I cooled off, I realized what a jerk I had been. I tried calling, but she didn't answer. I planned to apologize after I got home that evening. I was going to take her out to dinner, and I had bought her flowers...but then I got the call that I needed to come home."

"Oh, Keith." She placed her hand on his shoulder as she gazed into his misty eyes. "How did you ever get past that?"

"It took some time, but when I finally gave it all to God, knowing that there was nothing I could do to change what I had said, I was finally able to forgive myself. Since then, I haven't changed all that much as a person. I still get impatient when I'm rushed. I get angry at the boys and say stupid stuff I later regret. Mistakes are made daily, and daily I need to forgive and be forgiven. I know…beyond a shadow of a doubt, that had Kim lived that day, our marriage would have been just fine. I would have apologized, and she would have forgiven me. But for a long time after she died, I was like you, stuck in that one moment. I knew my kids needed me, so I didn't have a choice to remain there…and Carol…" He paused for a moment and gently rubbed her back. "Neither do you."

She laid her head on his chest and sighed. "I know. It's just…I just don't know where to start."

"Where to start? That's easy, you start right here and now by accepting the fact that you will never know for certain what might have happened had Paul lived, but you can allow yourself to imagine that everything would have been okay."

She nodded her head. "I guess I've just been stuck in that last moment like it was cement. I need to be free of it."

"You can, you just need to stop being afraid of letting go of it…you especially need to stop being afraid of me." His gaze was serious as he looked down at her.

"I'm not afraid of you," she whispered.

"Good." He leaned a little closer to her. "Listen, I don't know where this journey will take us, but I know where I want it to start." He moved a little closer. "I think right here and and now is as good a time as any." He then whispered near her ear, "Would it be okay…"

Her slight nod was the permission he needed to finally kiss her.

For him, it was a kiss that turned the page to a new chapter of his life. A chapter that he hoped would eventually lead to a happy ending. For her, the kiss had been like a jackhammer, breaking apart her hardened heart, allowing her to finally take that first step forward.

That one kiss led to another and then another, until they were both completely oblivious to the fact that it was now dark outside, that it was snowing, and that a waitress at the restaurant had just put the CLOSED sign in the window a few hours earlier than usual. Neither paid any attention as that same waitress, as well as the other staff, began heading out to their cars so that they could get home before the impending blizzard made it impossible to do so.

Chapter Sixteen

Keith ran his fingers through Carol's hair as she laid her head upon his chest. "I'd love to stay this way with you for a little while longer, but I gotta tell ya, Carol, I'm starving." He laughed. "Are you feeling better now?"

"Yes." She breathed a sigh of contentment. "But I'm hungry, too." She reluctantly pulled herself out of his arms. She then slid her hand across the window to remove the condensation. As soon as she could see outside, her mouth flew open in shock when she realized what was happening. "This snow is starting to come down really hard. We better try to get a weather report."

"They should know something inside the cafe. When Keith opened his door to get out, he didn't like the fact that the cafe's lights were turned off and there wasn't another car in sight.

"I thought you said they would still be open," she said worriedly once she too got out of the car.

"There's a note on the door. I'll go see what it says." He jogged up to the front door of the cafe and read, "Closed early due to impending blizzard."

He jogged back and said, "Sorry, you need to get back in the car."

"Why?" She asked as she got back inside. "What did the note say?"

"I think I have some bad news?"

"Hey, what happened to the glass half full attitude?" Carol said, not liking the look on his face.

"Well, let's see, how can I put a positive spin on the fact that the cafe is closed due to a blizzard?"

"That's impossible! Let me call my dad." She reached inside her purse and pulled out her cell phone. It didn't take her long to realize she had no service. "I've got nothing, how 'bout you?"

She watched as he checked his phone, then slowly began to shake his head. "No service." He looked out the window a few seconds, then turned back toward Carol. "I guess we just turn around and go home."

"No, we can't. Look how hard it's snowing...and the roads are now covered...the plows won't be up here for a few hours...or maybe even a few days! We're going to get stuck if we attempt to go back down the mountain."

"Nah, I think I can handle it. How bad could it get?"

"Keith, please. I know these mountains. They can be very dangerous in a snow storm. I can't believe this!" She had to wipe off her window again to get a good look outside. The wind had picked up, causing large snow drifts to form across the parking lot. "My dad is always watching the weather. I know he would have warned us if he had heard there was going to be a storm up here."

"Well, I guess like me, he didn't check on it today."

"I think we need to err on the side of caution and just stay here in the car and ride out the storm," Carol advised.

"We might freeze to death if we do that, but I do have another plan. A buddy of mine has a cabin up here. It's about a mile or so up the road. He let me and the boys use it last summer, so I know where he hides the key. There's no electricity or running water, but he has a gas stove, and a fireplace. We can stay there until the storm stops and the roads have been plowed."

"I don't know, Keith. My family will be worried sick. I wish there was a way to contact them."

"Unfortunately, there won't be. Having no cell service is the price you pay for the peace and tranquility you find up here."

"You're sure the cabin is just a mile from here?"

"Give or take."

"Keith...what does that mean?"

"It means I know the cabin is close by, but I'm not exactly sure how far. I still think it's our best option, though."

"You promise to drive slow?"

"I promise to go as slow as possible."

"Okay," she said as she nervously rubbed her hands along her legs. "Hopefully, our families won't worry too much."

"They're going to worry, but there's not much we can do about that now." He put the car in drive and just as soon as he pressed down on the gas pedal, the car began to slide from side to side. "Yep, it's pretty slick out."

"I don't know about this…" Carol anxiously looked out the window again.

"We'll be fine," he said as he made it out onto the main road. As he accelerated, the car pushed forward through the snow, but not without sliding here and there as they made their way further up the road.

"Please, slow down. We'll end up in a ditch if you try to keep up with this speed." Her knuckles were beginning to turn white from clenching her hands together.

"Yes, but if I go too slow, we won't be able to go at all. We'll lose traction."

After about fifteen minutes of rough driving, Carol feared they had already passed the cabin. It was so dark, it was hard to see anything. Finally, she looked out her window and managed to see the tin roof of a cabin that was a short a distance off the road. "Is that it?" She asked, pointing out her window.

"Yeah, that's it. I'm going to have to speed up a bit to be able to make it up that hill toward the cabin. We're probably going to slide some, but we'll be okay." He looked over at her and could see the fear in her eyes. "I promise, Carol, we'll be fine. I'm used to driving in the snow."

He was right, the trek up the hill was scary with the car's back tires often sliding around. When the car came to a quick halt, Keith looked over at her and saw that her eyes were shut tight, and she had covered her mouth with her hand to prevent from screaming.

"Hey," he said as he rubbed her knee. "We made it. You can open your eyes."

"Thank God," she whispered.

He took her hand in his as they walked toward the cabin. The snow was accumulating quite rapidly at this point, leaving a trail of deep footprints behind them. When they stepped up onto the porch, they stomped their feet several times to remove the snow from their shoes. Keith then reached up on top of the door ledge and pulled down the key. "I'm glad he didn't come up with a new hiding place."

He unlocked the door and reached for the flashlight that he knew would be hanging right next to the door. He turned it on, but didn't get much light. "Looks like this is going to need batteries soon. We better find the lanterns and hope that they still have kerosene in them."

It took them a while, but they finally had the cabin somewhat lit up with the two lanterns they had found. Though it was a small cabin with just the one room, it seemed to have everything that was needed. There wasn't a bed, but Keith said that the couch folded out to make a bed. There was a small table with two chairs, and on one side of the cabin was a make-shift kitchen with a small counter, a plastic tub for washing dishes, and a camp stove. There was only one cupboard and one drawer, so several pans and utensils were hanging from hooks on the wall.

"The fireplace is really big," Carol said. "But I don't see any wood."

"Kevin, my friend, likes to use the fireplace to do his dutch oven cooking. That's why it's so big. There is a woodshed out back. It's right next to the outhouse. I'll go out to get some wood. Why don't you see if there's any food we can make. I'll take that plastic tub there and get some snow, so we can have drinking water."

"Okay, but be careful. It's really coming down now."

"I will. If I'm not back in ten minutes, send the hounds out after me." He laughed.

"It's not funny, Keith." She shook her head. "Please…just be careful."

He started to leave, but when he still saw fear in her eyes, he walked over to her and took her hands in his. "It's going to be okay, Carol. We're safe." He leaned down and planted a soft kiss on her lips. "This is going to be nice. I'm looking forward to snuggling with you by the fire."

Carol shyly grinned. She had suspected that if she had ever agreed to go out with him, she'd be in love with him by the end of the evening. The only thing she had been wrong about was that the evening had only just begun.

"I'll be back in a few minutes. I might have to chop some logs, so it could take a little longer," he said as he opened the cabin door. A gust of icy air howled through the cabin putting a lot of force on the door which made it hard to close. "Man, this wind is ridiculous right now."

Carol walked over to help push the door shut. "I know I've already said this, but please be careful. Just take your time."

"I will. We'll have a nice fire before you know it."

With the door finally shut, Carol began to explore the corner that held the cooking items. She opened the cupboard and found several cans of chili, soups, vegetables and some kind of canned pasta dish. "Well, at least we won't starve," she said as she took down the chili, then went in search of a can opener, finding it inside the drawer.

Since Paul wasn't into camping, it had been a while since she had used a camp stove. As a child, her family had always gone camping during the summer. When she would ask Paul to take her and the children camping, he would just shake his head no and inform her that hotels had been made for a reason.

She was proud that she was able to get the stove started. She emptied the can of chili into a pot and while it began to heat up, she searched for some utensils. She found some paper bowls and plastic spoons and set them on the small table. She also found a candle and placed it in the center of the table and lit it. It wasn't much, but she liked the cozy feel of it.

After about twenty minutes, Keith still wasn't back. She wasn't too worried at that point since he had said he might have to chop the wood to make logs. After ten more minutes, she was worried enough that she went to the door and called out his name several times. However, it was practically impossible to hear anything other than the roar of the vicious wind. The snow was blowing so fiercely now that it was nearly a white-out condition. She couldn't even see the woodshed.

She began to feel the panic begin to rise inside of her. All she could think was, *Not again!* She waited five more minutes before she decided that she wasn't going to just sit there and do nothing. She zipped her coat clear up to her chin, opened the door, and walked out into the storm to find him.

Chapter Seventeen

"Oh, my goodness!" Abby exclaimed as she joined Magnus on the couch. "Those three did not want to go to sleep tonight!"

"They're overly tired from sledding. That was fun, but I'm definitely going to feel it tomorrow." He stretched his neck from one side to the other.

"That's why I don't go sledding anymore. I'm perfectly content to be the keeper of the hot chocolate." Abby chuckled.

"How was Blake when he went to bed?"

"He was fine, but he asked me if I loved you."

"That's an easy question to answer," he said as he patted her knee.

"Yes, it was." She covered his hand with hers. "I'm glad he didn't ask me about his father loving his mother. I wouldn't even know where to begin to answer that. I just don't understand why Paul would say that to Carol. It just breaks my heart to know they were having troubles in their marriage."

"I can't believe Paul would say what he did in front of the kids," Magnus added. "That doesn't sound like him at all."

"People change all the time, Magnus. The more I think about all the financial problems he was having, I suspect he was under a great deal of stress."

"I wish Carol had talked to us about this. I know she may not want to, but after talking with Blake and knowing how he was affected by their problems, I don't see how we can't. It's going to me a tough conversation to have with her."

"I know. I don't understand why she never said anything to us. Knowing Carol the way I do, though, I'm thinking she was embarrassed to admit she was having marital problems. Everyone always had such high expectations of her. She probably felt like she had failed in some way."

"I hope she hasn't felt that way. No marriage is perfect…" Magnus turned and looked at his wife. "Except maybe ours." He gave her a quick kiss, then said, "I thank God every day that you and I have had such a beautiful marriage."

"I am just as thankful," Abby said as she snuggled closer to him. "But it wasn't always easy. Don't you remember how insecure I was in the beginning of our marriage, especially after Carol was born."

"What I remember is that I married a very determined woman who wanted to make sure that her children knew how much they were loved. Carol has a lot of her mother in her. I know she'll be okay, and I know that her children are going to be just fine."

"Thank you, that's exactly what I needed to hear." She turned and kissed his cheek. She then stood up and walked over to the large picture window and turned on the Christmas lights. She then gazed outside for a few seconds longer to look for car headlights. "Magnus, what time is it?"

"It's a little after eight, why?"

"I know it's not all that late, but I guess I thought Carol would be home by now."

"I'm sure that they are having a wonderful time. The Smokey Moose doesn't close until eight, so I suspect they're heading home right now."

"Do you think the roads are okay?"

"Um…they should be." He thought about that for a second, then shook his head. "You know, I didn't even check the weather today."

"What?" She was surprised by that. "You always check the weather."

"That was before I had three rambunctious kiddos in the house." He laughed. "They are fun, but very exhausting."

"I know, I don't know how Carol did it all by herself last year."

"She's a strong woman. She always has been."

Abby looked outside again. "Well, the weather is fine here. We won't get any new snow for a few days yet."

"Things can be unpredictable up in the mountains, though. I'll just go to the office and check my weather apps on the computer."

He got up and went to his office and turned on his computer. It was the first time all day that he had turned it on, so it took a few minutes to get booted up. Just as soon as he logged on to a site that gave weather reports throughout the Pinecrest County and surrounding mountain areas, he felt as if his heart had stopped beating when he saw the bright red blizzard warning flash across the screen. "Dear, Lord," he whispered, still in shock by what he was seeing. "Abby! Come in here!"

"What is it?" She asked as she entered the room.

"This is bad. This is really bad!"

She walked up behind him and looked at the screen, seeing the warnings for herself. "Magnus? Where is that storm headed?"

"It's already there. Go call Carol and see if they're on their way home."

Abby called right away, but the phone went straight to voice mail. "Carol, when you get this message, please call us. I hope you're on your way home. There's a bad storm up there...please...just be careful."

After she hung up, she looked over at Magnus who was still studying the computer screen. "I think I'll call Lois and see if she's heard from Keith."

"That's a good idea."

Lois, who had just started to worry herself, was now scared to death after Abby called and informed her about the blizzard conditions up in the mountain. "I didn't even think about the weather. I was just so glad that he and Carol where having dinner together. This was the first time he's been out with any one since Kim died."

"It was also Carol's first time."

"She's a wonderful woman."

"We think very highly of Keith, as well."

"Do you think something happened to them?" Lois' voice cracked as she tried to keep from crying.

"I'm sure they are just fine. They are two very smart and highly capable people. If they ran into some trouble, they'll figure something out."

"Should we call someone? Maybe the police?"

"We can, just to see if they've heard anything, but I think we should give it a couple of hours. Magnus has a lot of contacts from when he was the mayor. If they're not home soon, he'll start making some phone calls."

"Please call me if you hear anything?" Lois pleaded.

"Of course, and you call me if you hear from Keith."

"I will. I guess there's not much we can do at this point."

"The most important thing we can do right now is pray," Abby reminded Lois.

"Yes, yes, you're right about that. I'll get to it right away! Good night, Abby."

"Good night, Lois. Try not to worry…and try to get some sleep."

"Thank you, but I won't go to bed until he's home."

"I know, me neither." She hung up the phone and went back to staring out the window. By ten o'clock she was pacing the floor, then at midnight, and they still weren't home, Magnus started making phone calls to county officials in charge of search and rescue.

Abby lost complete control of her emotions around two in the morning. Magnus tried to comfort her, but he also needed to be on the phone getting a crew together to go up to the mountains to begin searching for them. "Abby, I need you to be strong right now. The kids are going to need you when they wake up."

"I'm sorry...but if anything happens to her...Magnus, she has to be okay! I can't…"

"Shhh," he whispered as he wrapped his arms around her. "You can't allow yourself to think that way. God is with them. He will take care of them. Don't lose faith."

"I'll do my best, but it's so hard," she said as she wiped at her eyes. "I'm going to go call all the family. I know I'll wake them up, but we need to pray. Do you think I should I call Rev. Pickler, too?"

"I would call everyone," Magnus said. Keith and Carol are part of this community. You know how this town is when one of their own is in trouble. They'll rally around us giving us the support we need to get through this."

"Have you managed to get the county to agree to a search."

"There's a little bit of worry because the storm is still lingering. It's going to be a rough trip up there, but they should be leaving in a few hours."

"A few hours? Magnus, we need them to go now!"

"Abby," he said with a sigh. "It takes time. I'll hear something soon. In the meantime, I think you need to stay busy. Calling everyone is a good idea."

Abby was having a difficult time with her calls. As soon as she would tell them why she was calling, she'd start crying again. Especially, when she called Floyd and Nova's house.

Floyd had been the one to answer the early morning phone call. It didn't disturb his sleep, though, because he had already been up for hours. He was restless for some reason. He didn't know why, but when he got that way, he would go down to the kitchen, have a cup of one of his wife's relaxing teas, open his Bible, and begin to pray.

As soon he answered the phone, he didn't wait to hear who was calling before he spoke. "I don't know who this is calling at this hour, but I want you to know that I've been up for hours already praying about it."

"Oh, Floyd!" Abby cried. "Thank you! This is Abby…"

"Abby? Please don't tell me one of those little ones…"

"No..no, it's Carol...and Keith."

"Okay...what's going on?" He asked curiously.

"They went on a date yesterday. It was late afternoon…"

"Yes, I know. I think that they make a fine couple!"

"Yes, but…" She began to sob.

"Honey, just take your time," he tried to soothe her the best he could over the phone.

"Floyd...they never came home."

"What do you mean they never came home?"

"They went to dinner at the Smokey Moose...up in the mountains."

"There's a blizzard up there right now!"

"They didn't know."

"Magnus didn't know? He's the weather guy in this town. He always knows…"

"He didn't check. We had plans with the children...things have changed in our house. It's nice, but we don't always..."

"You don't have to say anything more. I understand. I've got grandchildren of my own. They keep us in a tizzy, don't they?"

"Yes, they do."

"So, tell me what's happening with Keith and Carol."

"We can't get a hold of them on their phones. We notified the police, but they've told us we need to wait 24 hours. But until then, we have to do something…" She began to choke up again.

"Of course, we will pray. Have you called Rev. Pickler yet?"

"Yes, he was going to start the prayer chain."

"Well, I'll take over your calls from here on out. Have you called all your family?"

"Most of them. I still need to call Charles and Irene and...um...it wouldn't hurt to call Carol's in-laws. I think they would want to know. I better call them, though. They don't know you."

"I think you need to get a couple of hours of sleep. Those little ones are going to be getting up soon. I have Charles' number, but I need the number for the in-laws."

"Thank you, Floyd. I was dreading that call."

"Why?"

"They aren't really...I don't know, it's just they haven't been all that pleased with our family."

"Now, who in their right mind wouldn't just love your family?"

"They weren't particularly pleased that Paul married Carol. Now that he's gone, they prefer not to have anything to do with us. But...those precious children are their grandchildren, too. I think they would be upset if we didn't tell them about Carol being missing."

"Of course, they would. Don't you worry. I'm happy to call them for you."

"Floyd, it won't be easy."

"That's just the way I like it!" He laughed. "Now, let me just get a pen to jot down their number." Once he was back, he wrote down the number and once again instructed Abby to go get some sleep. As soon as he hung up, he dialed the number for Charles and Irene, Abby's brother and sister-in-law. Charles was the previous pastor at St. Timothy Lutheran Church and was used to getting calls in the middle of the night. He let Floyd know that he and his wife, Irene, would head over to Magnus' house right away. Floyd then dialed the number for Winslow and Cecily.

Winslow answered the phone with a gruff voice. "Who is this? Do you know what time it is?"

"I'm sorry to disturb your rest, but I am a friend of Carol Brunswick. My name is Floyd Emerson. Carol's mother, Abby, thought I should call and let you all know that Carol is in some trouble..."

"Trouble? What kind of trouble?" Winslow was fully awake now. He sat up in bed and shifted the phone to his other hand.

"She went up to the mountains on a date and hasn't returned."

"Winslow? Who's that on the phone?" Cecily asked as she propped herself up in the bed.

Winslow covered the receiver with his hand. "Someone named Floyd...a friend of Carol's. She was on a date and hasn't come home yet."

"Give me that phone!" She yanked it out of his hand.

"A date, huh? That figures. Our son has been in the grave for only a year and she's out flaunting around with other men."

"Who am I speaking with?" Floyd was confused by the change of voice.

"This is Cecily Brunswick. My son, Paul, was married to that...that...woman!" She growled into the phone. "Tell me exactly why you are calling!"

"Okay, well, Mrs. Brunswick, it is highly possible that Carol is trapped somewhere in a blizzard. Carol's mother, Abby Engle, thought you would want to know."

"Is this a crank call?" She stated loudly.

"No! This is not a crank call!" Floyd said angrily. He rarely lost his patience with people, but this woman was downright aggravating. "Because of the children, we thought you'd want to know so that you could pray."

"Listen to me. This is very important. Is she still wearing her wedding ring?"

"What? Did you hear me state the fact that she is missing. She didn't come home last night, and we fear that she may be trapped somewhere in a terrible storm."

"That ring belonged to my mother. I want it back! You tell Carol..."

"Hold your horses, young lady!" Floyd said. "I don't know what you're talking about. I only called to inform you that Carol is in possible danger. As the grandparents of her children, we thought you would want to know."

"I don't care one bit about that woman. I want my ring back. If something happens to her, you let Magnus and Abby know that we'll file for custody of the children. Lord knows it will be work for us, but we'll make sure they get the right kind of upbringing and education."

"Ma'am, I'm a God-fearing man who served as a pastor for many years. I don't swear, I don't drink, and I don't wish anyone harm, ever….but I tell you what…you are trying my patience something fierce! I'm going to hang up this phone, but before I do, I have to tell you that you are going on my daily prayer list of cantankerous people that the good Lord needs to get His hands on to straighten out before you meet him face to face at the pearly gates."

"How dare you…" she hissed.

With that, Floyd hung up the phone and shook his head back and forth. "Lord, help 'em!"

"Floyd? Were you talking on the phone?" His wife, Nova, asked as she entered the kitchen with her robe and slippers on.

"Yes, dear. I'm afraid there's some bad news in the community. We're being called upon to pray."

"Oh, no! What happened?"

"Keith and Carol went on a date up in the mountains yesterday afternoon. They never came home."

"There's a storm up there right now," Nova said as she poured herself a cup of hot water, then dropped in a tea bag.

"Yes, from my understanding, they weren't aware of the weather report. I'm afraid they are trapped up there. I just hope they had provisions in the car."

"Were they in that sports car that Keith likes to drive?"

"I imagine so."

"Why do men buy cars like that? They are so impractical."

"That's probably why...men like to do impractical. But that is neither here nor there. Those two are good folks with children who are depending on them. If they aren't home, we can be assured that there is a very good reason for it. I suspect the roads got pretty bad up there real fast."

"Oh, dear, Jesus." Nova shook her head. "May God have mercy on 'em."

"He will. That's the only certainty we have right now."

"It sounded like you had raised your voice down here. That's what woke me up."

"I'm sorry about that, dear. I was making some calls for Abby. It seems that our sweet Carol has got herself a persnickety mother-in-law. Would you believe the woman was more concerned about Carol's wedding ring than she was about Carol!" He found himself getting angry again.

"A ring? Why would she care about that?"

"I don't know." He shook his head. "I'm thinking that I'd love to sit down and have a good long chat with that woman."

"Uh oh...I know what that means," Nova said with a grin. "What are the names of Carol's in-laws?"

Floyd looked down at the paper where he had written down the information Abby gave him. "Let's see...their names are Winslow and Cecily Brunswick."

"Well, as we pray for Carol and Keith, I think we should add their names to our prayers as well."

"Oh, yes! I already told them we'd be doing just that!" Floyd nodded his head. "Mama," he said as he took his wife's hand, "now is as good a time as any." He bowed his head. "Lord, you know the circumstances. You know what it is needed. We believe you will provide. Calm the hearts and minds of all those who are afraid. May we all put our trust in you, especially Carol and Keith...and while you're fixin' all the messes we get ourselves into, please take some time to soften the heart of that bitter, old..."

"Floyd!" Nova scolded.

"All right, all right! We ask for your grace and mercy for Winslow and Cecily...if it be your will, send those folks my way. I'd love to spend some quality time gettin' to know them better."

Chapter Eighteen

"Keith! Keith!" Carol screamed as loud as she could, but her voice was like a whisper in comparison to the howling wind. It was slow going and brutal as she maneuvered her way through the deep snow. She didn't have on snow boots or gloves, so her feet and hands were stinging from the frigid air. Several times she would bring her cupped hands up to her mouth and blow her breath on them, trying desperately to warm her frozen fingers.

She wished now that she had gone for practical instead of style with her choice of coat. The one she had on was warm enough for going from the car to the restaurant as was originally planned, but it definitely was not a coat to be outside in for too long, and it certainly was not a coat one should wear to try to fend off an unexpected blizzard. Grabbing a hat and gloves wasn't even an afterthought as she was getting ready this afternoon. She now knew that she would learn from this experience that it was always best to be prepared for unexpected weather versus trying to make an impression on a guy who had, at the moment, seemed to have vanished into thin air.

"Keith!" She yelled again. "Where are you?"

Her foot hit a fallen branch hidden under the snow, causing her to lunge forward. She cried out in pain as her hip hit hard on the branch. She laid there in the snow for several seconds, trying to catch her breath. It had been a while since she had been up in the mountains where the air was thin. Her lungs felt like they were on fire. "God, I need your help," she prayed. She had whispered that same prayer many times over the last year.

"Keith! Please! Answer me!" She yelled, as she managed to get herself up off the ground.

She stopped walking and tried to listen for him, but she could only hear the sound of the wind now mixed with her labored breath. She walked a few more feet and listened again.

Finally, in the distance, she heard a muffled sound. Driven by hope, she pushed forward. "Keith, is that you?"

Again, she heard the sound and tried to figure out which direction it was coming from. Her eyes strained through the darkness to try to make out the woodshed. The lanterns inside the cabin gave her a little light, but visibility was almost impossible. She looked in every direction, but still couldn't see Keith or anything that resembled a shed. All she could see was what appeared to be a small structure that had collapsed into a pile of rubble. That's when it dawned on her that the pile of rotted wood was most likely the woodshed.

"Keith!" She frantically screamed as she quickened her pace as much as she was able. As she got closer to the pile of wood, the muffled sound got louder, and she thought she could see a person propped up against a tree.

Her emergency room nursing skills kicked in. She no longer concentrated on how her frozen limbs were screaming at her. She was now fully focused on saving a life. When she reached him, she fell to the ground next to him. "Keith! What's wrong? Are you hurt?"

"Thank God you came," he said with a strained voice.

"What happened?"

"A gust of wind hit the woodshed at just the right spot. I was just about to chop a log when part of the structure fell against me. I'm afraid I hit my ankle instead."

"With the ax?" She looked down at his feet. Though it was dark, she was able to make out a dark spot forming on the snow. "Keith, you're bleeding!"

He nodded his head. "I barely made it to this tree. I don't know if I can walk to get back to the cabin."

"Do you think you can stand up?"

"I don't know. I'm going to need your help."

It took several attempts, but he was finally able to stand with his arm wrapped around her shoulders for support. When he began to sway, she asked, "Are you dizzy?"

"A little. I've lost quite a bit of blood."

"It's going to be tough getting back to the cabin, so work with me, okay. Don't you dare fall in the snow! I'll be so mad at you if you do!"

He attempted to laugh at that, but the pain was too intense for him to form anything other than a grimace.

It was maybe only 50 yards from the woodshed to the cabin, but Carol felt like she had just run a marathon by the time they slowly made their way up the steps and into the cabin. She got him over to the couch and helped him sit down. When she pulled off his shoes, he cried out in pain. "Careful," he said through clinched teeth.

"I'm sorry. I don't want to cause you any more pain, but I've got to see how bad it is."

Thankfully, the gash wasn't too deep. She did her best to clean the wound, she then cut a dish towel into strips and carefully wrapped them around his foot. "This should stop the bleeding. You might need some stitches, but it's not as bad as it could have been."

"Thank you for coming out to look for me."

"You were gone a little longer than I thought you should be. I figured something must have happened."

"Yeah...and unfortunately, I didn't get any wood."

"I'll have to go out and get some."

"You can't go back out there. It's too dangerous."

"Freezing to death is dangerous, too." She didn't wait for him to protest further. She turned and went back out into the cold.

Several minutes later, she was back with a stack of logs in her arms. "I'll light these, but I'll need to go back out and get some more so we have enough to get through the night." She turned toward the kitchen area to get the matches. When she turned back around, she saw that he had laid his head back against the couch and had closed his eyes. She rushed back to him, placed her hands on both sides of his face and sternly yelled, "Wake up, Keith! Wake up!"

When his eyes fluttered open, she sighed with relief. "You scared me."

"I'm okay. Just a little woozy. I think I need to eat something. Did you find anything to eat in that cupboard?"

"Yeah. Let me get this fire started first, then I'll bring you something to eat."

Carol stacked the logs and put some paper kindling underneath them. She was relieved when the logs began to smoke. After a few minutes, she had a nice fire going. She then went over to start the stove up again to reheat the chili.

Keith turned his head to look over at the kitchen area and said, "Thanks, Carol. You're doing an amazing job by the way. I think I'm a lot luckier than I thought I was when you agreed to come work with me. You're a good nurse."

"Thank you. I've always liked taking care of people."

"You did more than just take care of me. You saved my life." He said more seriously. "If you hadn't of come out when you did…"

"I just wish I had gone out looking for you sooner."

"It's okay. You got there in time."

"I hope so. You might have hypothermia."

"I don't think so. I'm already starting to warm up. That's a really great fire you started."

Carol walked back to the couch with the bowl of chili. "I'll get you some water after all that snow melts. Do you need me to feed you?"

He laughed, realizing she was serious. "Thankfully, I still have full use of my hands."

She handed him the bowl then went back to get a bowl for herself. Together, they sat on the couch with a sleeping bag thrown over their legs. They watched the fire while eating the overly spicy chili which warmed them all the way to their toes.

"This stuff is awful! Certainly not something you want to eat on a first date!" Carol said with a chuckle.

"Ah, ha! So, this is a date, isn't it?"

"Yeah, I guess it is." She looked at him and smiled. "I will admit that even though this date is far from perfect, I'm glad to be here with you."

He placed his finished bowl on the small table next to the couch. He then wrapped an arm around her shoulders. "What do you mean far from perfect? I think it's absolutely perfect. It's going to be hard to top it."

"Well, let's see…a blizzard, frozen toes and fingers, a gash on your foot, no cell phone service, no bathroom, no electricity, and a flaming hot bowl of chili out of a can...yes, I'd say you can't get much better than this!" Though the evening was worthy of tears, she was glad that she was able to laugh about it.

"Don't forget snuggling with the Corn Queen by the fire." He pulled her closer to his side.

"I won't ever forget, Keith," she said quietly as she rested her head on his shoulder. "Today has been a fresh start for me."

"Yeah, it has been for me, too."

Chapter Nineteen

The sound of the cabin door opening woke Carol from her restless sleep. She pushed aside the sleeping bag, and sat up on the couch and looked around the room. She frowned when she saw Keith coming back inside the cabin.

"Were you outside?"

"Yeah, I went to use the outhouse."

"Keith, you shouldn't have gone out there by yourself."

"I know, but you were sleeping, and I didn't want to wake you."

He hobbled over to the couch and sat down next to her.

"How are you feeling?" She asked as she reached up and felt his head to make sure he didn't have a fever.

Neither had slept very much during the night. The pain in Keith's ankle had kept him awake most the night, and Carol spent the night keeping her eye on Keith. She was worried about him getting an infection."

"My ankle still hurts, but I'm able to walk on it now. I was wondering if you were hungry."

"I'm famished! Bacon and eggs sounds good to me," she said with a hint of sarcasm.

He stood up then and limped back over to the cupboard. "Sorry, no bacon or eggs in here, but I can pop open a couple of cans of chicken noodle soup. That always cures what ails ya."

"Come sit back down, Keith. I can make it. You need to get off your feet."

"I'm fine, besides you've been waiting on me all night. I think it's my turn to take care of you now." He reached for the matches, then lit the stove.

"Are you sure you're okay?"

"I feel like a million bucks!" He grinned at the obvious lie.

"No, you don't...but I'm glad to see that you can stand without support. How's the snow looking outside?"

"There's just some light flurries out there, but thankfully the wind has stopped. It's actually a beautiful sunrise."

"Your car…"

"Buried."

"I was afraid of that. Hopefully, the snow plows will be up here soon."

She stretched out on the couch again and pulled the sleeping bag up around her shoulders. "I'm sure my parents are a wreck by now. I can't imagine how they explained this to the kids."

"I know. I was thinking about Lois and the boys this morning. I'm sure Lois is doing her best to keep them from worrying about me."

"Even if they send people up to search for us, do you think they'll come up this way?" Carol asked. "Our tire tracks are probably buried by now."

"I'm hoping they'll see the smoke from the cabin."

"Oh! That reminds me, we're going to need more wood." She started to get up again.

"Don't worry about it. I'll get it after we eat."

"No, you won't! You need to get off that foot. Why is it that doctors are always the worst patients?"

"I don't know. We're not supposed to get hurt or sick, I suppose."

"That would only be if you weren't human."

He used his bare hand to try to move the pan off the camp stove, not realizing how hot the pot would be. As he quickly pulled his hand away and reached for a hot pad, he said, "I'm definitely human! By the way, the soup is ready."

Carol stood up and rolled her shoulders to try to get some of kinks out. It seemed as if every muscle in her body was screaming at her. However, she still managed to smile when she noticed how rumpled and completely adorable Keith looked standing over the stove, stirring the soup.

"I hope I'm never trapped again during a storm, but I gotta say, Keith, that if I am, I hope you're with me…without the gash in your ankle, of course."

He looked up at her and smiled. "You've been amazing, Carol. You do well under pressure."

"I wouldn't have survived the ER if I didn't know how to remain calm. I'll share a secret with you, though. I'm always a nervous wreck on the inside," she said as she sat down at the small table.

"Well, you could have fooled me." He poured the soup into two bowls and handed her a spoon.

"Thanks." She noticed then that he didn't wear his wedding ring. "When were you able to take your ring off?"

He looked down at his ring finger for a few moments without saying anything.

"I'm sorry, I shouldn't have asked that. It's really none of my business."

"No, it's fine. It's just sometimes I forget that I'm not still wearing it. I took it off during the funeral. I placed it in the coffin with Kim."

"Why?" She looked at him curiously.

"Our vows were until death do us part. The way I saw it, death had parted us."

She nodded her head. "I guess I see your point. That must have been terribly hard to do, though."

"It was, but it seemed like the right thing for me to do. I think that it helped me to understand the reality of her death. I don't know if that makes any sense or not, but it helped me to be able to move on after a while."

"I just took mine off a couple of days ago. Maybe that's why I feel the way I do now."

"Oh? How do you feel?"

"Like maybe I could...you know…"

"No, I don't know." He chuckled. "What are you saying?"

"You know...maybe date someone...see where it leads...you know?"

"Oh…I see." He smiled. When he saw her cheeks begin to blush, he reached out and took one of her hands in his. "I feel the same way."

"If there ever is a next time, I don't want such an expensive ring, though."

"I noticed your ring right away. It had a beautiful diamond on it."

"It had belonged to Paul's grandmother. His mother called the other day and asked that I give it back to her. At first, I told her no, but I've been thinking that maybe I should give it to her."

"First of all, I don't like this woman. I want to get that off my chest. Regardless if it was in the family or not, it was given to you as a symbol of Paul's love and commitment. It's up to you to decide what to do with it."

"I know. I just think that maybe giving it back will help mend our relationship. I may never be good friends with her, but I want my children to know and love all their grandparents. Right now things are so awkward between me and my in-laws. If I keep the ring, it may just make matters worse."

"Just remember you have what's most important, your children. If your mother-in-law is more concerned about a ring than seeing her grandchildren, I say she is in need of some serious help."

"You're right," she said as she nodded her head. She then stood up and walked over to the tub that they were using to melt snow for drinking water. "You know what I think?"

"What's that?"

"Forget all this half full, half empty stuff. We both could use a full cup of water." She chuckled as she filled their cups all the way to the top. "Though, I must say, as thankful as I am that we have water, I could really go for a hot cup of coffee right now."

"I echo that remark! A nice hot cup of coffee is definitely at the top of my list of things I want to do as soon as I get home."

"I really do hope we are able to get out of here sometime today."

"Speaking of going home," Keith said. "When we do get back home, and let's say I was to call you and ask you to go to dinner or to maybe just go have a cup of coffee together…what would your answer be?"

"My answer would be yes, Keith." Her smile was genuine.

"I was hoping you would say that because I was wondering…Carol, would you like to go steady with me?"

"Steady?" She laughed. "What exactly does that mean, anyway?"

"It's a term my parents often used. In high school they always used to say that Kim and I were 'going steady.' I didn't know what it meant it either, but I suppose it means you'd be my girlfriend."

She could feel her cheeks begin to blush again. Her heart began to pound in a steady rhythm, and the smile on her face widened. She felt like a teenager being asked out for the first time. "This is so crazy! A few days ago I was so mad at you. I thought you were the worst human on the planet."

"You did?" He pretended to be shocked by that. "Gosh, I thought you really liked me at first." He grinned at her and gave her a quick wink.

She began to laugh. "I suspect you thought I was a little annoying too, didn't you?"

"I thought you were stubborn, infuriating, but...extremely beautiful."

She lowered her eyes, embarrassed by the compliment. "I haven't been called beautiful in a very long time."

"Well, you should have been. You are a beautiful woman, Carol. Both inside and out...but you haven't answered whether or not you'll go steady with me."

She looked up at him and stared into his eyes for several moments. She then leaned across the small table and kissed him on the cheek.

"Was that a yes?"

She answered by nodding her head.

He took both of her hands in his and gently began to pull her closer so that he could kiss her this time. However, when he heard a loud roaring sound, he quickly shifted his head toward the window. "Please tell me that's what I think it is!" He stood up, pulling Carol with him as he went to the door.

Once outside, they both shivered from the cold, so he put his arm around her and pulled her close to his side. From the front porch they could see a snowplow slowly making its way up the main road. They joyfully began to wave their arms in the air and didn't stop until the plow turned and began to plow the road that lead up to the cabin.

<h1 style="text-align:center">Chapter Twenty</h1>

"What kind of car is this, Winslow? I said to get something with four wheel drive!" Cecily said angrily as she watched Winslow put their luggage inside the small trunk of the compact car.

"This is all they had, dear. It will have to do."

"We'll probably slide all the way to that ridiculous town!"

"I'm not sure why you insisted we come all this way unannounced like this. I think we should have called first."

"If Carol knows I'm coming, she'll hide my mother's ring from me. I'm not leaving without it."

"I want you to know that this is your fight, Cecily. I want no part of it!"

"Of course, you don't! You never take my side on anything!" she yelled as she opened the door and tried to maneuver herself into the seat. She threw her purse into the back seat and yelled again, "I barely have room for my legs!"

"We can wait until tomorrow to get a larger car if you'd like. It would probably be safer than driving in this one. It looks like there is fresh snow on the road."

"I will not stay one day longer than necessary!"

"Okay, then stop complaining about how small this car is!" Winslow said with a raised voice after he slid inside the car. He then slammed the door and started the ignition, questioning himself once again as to why he allowed his wife to talk him into this trip. He wanted to see his grandchildren, that's why. He missed them terribly.

As he made his way out of the airport parking lot, he said, "I know you're in a hurry to get there and leave again, but I was hoping we could spend a little time with the children. It might be a while before we see them again."

"I doubt Carol will even let us see them."

"Of course, she will! Carol never denied us seeing the children. If I recall, she often invited us to come over for dinner. You just always had other plans."

"Winslow, our son would still be alive if he hadn't insisted on marrying...that...that...country bumpkin! His death is all her fault!"

He turned his head toward her, giving her a sharp look. "She is not to blame for Paul's death!" When Cecily turned her face toward the window, he added, "You didn't tell her that, did you?"

When she remained silent, Winslow's voice got louder, "Cecily! Did you tell her that she was to blame for Paul's death?"

"Yes!" she snapped. "But she should have known I was talking out of grief. For goodness' sake, Winslow, we lost our only child! So, what does she do? She up and moves hundreds of miles away from us taking our grandchildren with her."

"You mean taking the ring with her?" he growled.

"Well, yes, and that, too. She didn't have to move, though. She could have gone back to work. I'm sure she was just being lazy."

"It would have cost her too much to put the children in daycare. Nurses don't make that much money. We could have helped her out, though. If I recall, it was you who said not to give her a dime."

"And why should we?"

"Because Paul would have wanted us to."

"I highly doubt that. Paul was about to file for a divorce."

"What? How do you know that?"

"Because I was the one that helped him with all the paperwork."

"You did what?" He couldn't believe what he was hearing.

"He was extremely busy, Winslow. His practice took up most of his time. So, yes, I helped him by finding a good lawyer and getting the process started." She sniffed a few times, then pulled out a tissue from her purse and dabbed at her nose with it.

"It sounds to me like you were interfering in their marriage. Did you ever suggest that they go to counseling?"

"Of course, not! Everyone would have known they were having problems then. Can you imagine the talk at the country club?"

He looked at his wife with complete astonishment. He knew that she could be vindictive, but he had no idea she would ever stoop this low. "Paul loved Carol. I know that was hard for you to accept."

"He did not love her! Especially, not after I told him…" She caught herself before saying anything more.

"Cecily! What did you do?"

"Nothing, really." She turned and looked out the window again to avoid eye contact.

"You did something! Now you tell me what you did right now, or I'm pulling this car over."

"Then what will you do? Sit and freeze to death?"

"No...I'll help you out of the car and leave you here to freeze to death!"

"You wouldn't do that!"

He pulled off the road and stopped the car. "Do you really want to push me on that right now?" He scowled at her.

"Fine, if you must know, all I did was let Paul know what kind of a woman he had married."

"Oh, really? So you told him how fortunate he was to have someone like Carol as his wife?"

"No, that's not even close to what I told him. He needed to know what she did all day while he was at work."

"What she did all day? The woman had three young children at home! She was exhausted."

"Yes, but I'm sure she had friends over all day to sit around and gossip with...maybe even friends of the opposite sex."

"She did no such thing, and you know it!" His face was beginning to turn beet red from anger.

"You need to calm down, dear. You know what the doctor said about your heart."

He took several deep breaths, then pulled back out onto the highway. He didn't speak again.

Cecily hated the silent treatment. She knew he was mad, and she also knew she needed to let him calm down before talking to him again. However, at the moment, she didn't care. She looked at her husband and said, "I just want my mother's ring back. There's no crime in that, is there?"

"It's not your ring. It belongs to Carol. She can do with it what she wants," he hissed, still too angry to speak calmly.

"If that's the case, you might as well just turn this car around. I have nothing to say to her."

"Oh, we're still going. We have plenty to say to her... at least I do."

"Like what?" She glared at him.

"Like, please forgive me." He turned to his wife then. "I should have put my foot down with your constant interference in her life. I should have told her how happy I was that Paul found her and gave me the best daughter I could ever have. There's so much I should have said and done...I only hope that she will find it in her heart to forgive me."

Chapter Twenty-one

"Magnus!" Abby shouted. "They found them!" She held the phone out to him. "The police chief is on the phone for you!"

She was crying tears of joy as she handed the phone to her husband. He held the phone in one hand and wrapped his other arm around his wife and pulled her close to his side. "Hello...yes, I heard. Thank the good Lord!...Are they hurt?…Good, good...okay...let them know we'll meet them over at the hospital."

"Hospital?" Abby whispered. "Why? Are they hurt?"

Magnus shook his head while he continued to listen to the chief. "Thanks again. We'll see you soon!" He hung up the phone then pulled his wife into his arms and for just a few moments he finally allowed himself to cry. "They're fine. Keith has a cut on his ankle that's why they are heading to the hospital. Otherwise they are just fine."

"Where were they?"

"They got caught in the storm. Keith knew that his friend had a cabin near by, so he drove there instead of driving home. I'm not sure how he hurt his foot, but they're fine. They're just fine," he repeated, needing to hear himself say it again.

"Oh, my goodness. I can't even imagine what they've been through." She pulled herself out of his arm then took his hand in hers. "We better go tell the kids."

They found the children sitting on the couch watching television. Abby had hoped the cartoon would distract them. All three had woke up this morning wondering where their mother was at. Only Zoe had cried for her, though. The other two were concerned, but Magnus and Abby did their best to assure them that they would be just fine. As long as they could keep them distracted, they didn't ask too many questions, but both Magnus and Abby could see the fear in their eyes, especially with Blake.

"We have news!" Abby chirped. "Your mother and Mr. Bradley are safe and are on their way home!"

Blake jumped to his feet and ran to his grandfather. Lizzie ran to her grandmother and grabbed hold of her legs, while Zoe reached out her arms wanting to be held. Magnus and Abby both sighed with relief as they held the children, silently thanking God for his protection.

"Now, who wants to go to the hospital to see Mommy?" Magnus asked.

"Is Mommy hurt?" Lizzie asked.

"No, your mother is okay. She was very brave and spent the entire night nursing Mr. Bradley who did get a little bit hurt, but the Chief assured me that he was okay, too."

"Let's go!" Blake ran to the door.

"Not so fast, kiddo!" Abby ran after him. "It's snowing out there. We need coats, hats, gloves...the works."

"Fine," Blake mumbled as he dropped his head.

"Hey chin up, buddy," Magnus said. Your mother will only want to see smiles from you three, okay?"

After they were suited up for the cold, they drove over to the hospital. They pulled into the parking lot at the same time that an ambulance was pulling up with its sirens blaring. The sound scared Zoe, making her cry. Lizzie and Blake feared that their mother was inside. "Is Mommy in there?" Blake asked.

"No. They were going to ride back in the chief's car," Magnus answered. "I see it parked over there."

"But who is in the ambulance?" Lizzie asked.

"I don't know, honey," Abby said. "An ambulance brings people to the hospital who are in need of medical care. Someone must be sick or hurt."

As they made their way to the front entrance of the hospital, they could hear a woman screaming and crying near the ambulance. "What's wrong with that woman?" Blake asked as he turned his head to look in the direction where the ambulance had parked. At that point, the EMTs were pulling a gurney out of the back door of the ambulance. They then began to push the person up to the entrance of the ER department. The screaming woman was following close behind.

"I don't know, buddy. She sounds very upset, doesn't she?" Magnus looked down at Blake, but he was gone. As he looked around, he saw him running toward the woman. "Blake! No! Come back!" Magnus yelled. He handed Zoe to Abby. "Take the girls inside. I'll go get him."

"Grandma?" Blake asked as he ran up behind the woman who was crying uncontrollably.

She abruptly turned around after hearing the child's voice. "Blake," she barely whispered. "Is that you?"

"Yep, it's me!" He said cheerfully.

"You've grown some," she said with tears forming in her eyes. She slowly held out her arms, and Blake happily ran into them. "Oh, sweetheart! I've missed you so much."

"Cecily?" Magnus was confused. "I didn't realize you were coming to town. Was that Winslow on the gurney?"

"Hello, Magnus," she said as she released Blake from her tight hug. "Winslow had a heart attack…and…" She closed her eyes and shook her head. "I'm sorry, I'm…I'm just so overwhelmed right now. I need to go be with him."

"Yes, of course. If you need a place to stay, we'll make room for you at the house."

"I've already made a reservation at the motel in town, but thank you." She reached for Blake and gave him another hug. "I'll see you and your sisters soon, but Grandma needs to go check on Grandpa right now."

"Okay," Blake said as he stepped back. He then slipped his hand into Magnus', feeling nervous and scared for his other grandfather.

They both stood there for a moment and watched Cecily chase after the gurney. Neither of them knew what to say. Finally, Magnus said, "Well, Blake, I'm not sure what's going on, but this is turning out to be a very interesting day."

"Yeah…it's kind of crazy."

Magnus laughed as he nodded his head. "Yeah, I'd have to agree with you there, buddy. Come on, let's go find your mother."

It had been a tearful reunion for all, especially for Carol. The moment she saw her children, she ran to them and gathered all three in her arms. "I can't tell you how happy I am to see you all," she said with tears streaming down her face.

"Mama! Guess what?" Blake said, grinning from ear to ear.

"What?" Carol asked.

"Grandma from Chicago is here!"

"Here? In Snowflake Falls?" She looked over at her parents for confirmation.

Magnus nodded his head. "It seems we have a lot to talk about, sweetheart."

Chapter Twenty-two

"Hello!" Cecily called out as she rang the bell that was sitting on the counter in the lobby of the Snowflake Falls Motel.

"Just a sec'!" A voice called out from the backroom.

While Cecily waited, she looked around the small motel lobby with a sour look on her face. She had imagined the place would be low scale, but she never imagined it would be downright tacky.

The lobby was painted in a peachy color that clashed with the dark, red carpet and yellow counter tops. Tall plastic plants in green, bucket-like pots filled every corner of the room. A metal TV tray held a coffee pot along with cream and sugar. The leftover morning coffee in the pot had left a pungent aroma in the air that turned Cecily's stomach.

What was I thinking making a reservation here? She thought as she rested an elbow on the counter and waited rather impatiently to get checked in.

Her eyebrows involuntarily moved upward when an elderly woman with a head full of tightly permed curls popped her head around the corner. "I just need one more minute. I seem to have gotten myself in quite a pickle."

"Are you in need of some assistance?" Cecily reluctantly asked, hoping the woman would say no.

"Um...if you don't mind. I could use another set of hands."

Cecily, unsure of what she had just gotten herself into, hesitantly walked around the counter then entered through the doorway where she could get a better look at the woman who was standing near a table that was full of cakes, pies, cookies, casseroles, and salads. In her hands she held a stack of casserole containers that she was trying to make room for on the table.

"If you could take the top two casserole dishes, I think you'll find room for those in the freezer just over there." Since she didn't have a finger to point, she moved her entire body in the

164

direction of an upright freezer while continuing to balance the dishes in her hands.

The woman sighed with relief when Cecily removed two of the containers. "Phew! Thank you so much. I was afraid that I was about to drop them all."

"There is a lot of food here," Cecily said as she attempted to squeeze the dishes into the very full freezer. "Are you having a party?" She was suddenly worried there would be a lot of noise during the night when she desperately needed to sleep.

"No, all this food is for a woman who is going through a very difficult time right now." She was able to find a little space on the table where she placed the remainder of the dishes she had still been holding. "People here in town just wanted to show their love and support for her."

"Oh, I see. I suppose that was very thoughtful of them."

"Yes, the poor thing was traveling here to see her grandchildren for Christmas. Her husband suffered a heart attack just as they were pulling into town!" The woman threw her hands into the air. "I just can't imagine how horrifying that would be."

Cecily's mouth dropped open. "Do you know the woman's name?"

"Let's see…" The woman looked down at a piece of paper attached to one of the dishes. "Ah, yes, here we are. Her name is Cecily Brunswick. She is the dear, sweet mother-in-law of one of our most beloved community members."

Cecily placed a hand on her chest and declared, "I'm Cecily Brunswick. Are you saying all this food is for me?" She began to shake her head. "I don't understand."

The woman gasped before she enthusiastically lunged forward and wrapped her arms around Cecily, causing her to take a few steps back. She would have fallen over, but the woman then gripped Cecily's shoulders like a vice. "You poor, poor woman! How tragic to have such a thing happen so close to Christmas. Please, come into my apartment and have a seat."

Cecily wasn't given time to respond. She was quickly ushered into the small apartment attached to the motel lobby and was then forced down into an over-stuffed chair. She sank deep into the cushion, causing her bottom to be aggressively poked by one of the springs. "Oh, goodness!" She tried to get back up, but it was as if the chair had swallowed her up.

"Oops! Sorry about that." The woman giggled. "I keep meaning to have Earl fix those springs."

"Earl?" Cecily asked as she shifted in the chair to find a less painful spot.

"My heavens! Where are my manners! My name is Velma Jones. My husband, Earl, and I own this motel. Word spread quickly about your tragic circumstances, and the good folks of Snowflake Falls began to do what they do best"

"What would that be? Pray?" She remembered that was the reason why that Floyd person had called her the other night.

"Yes, we pray, but we also cook and bake! Usually we pray while we're cooking and baking." She giggled as she waved her hands in the direction of another table packed full cakes and pies. "I guarantee you will not starve while you wait for your husband to get better."

Cecily opened her mouth, but nothing came out. She was too stunned by what she was hearing. It was unbelievable that all this food had been made just for her. Finally she managed to ask, "How would anyone know...I mean I hardly know anyone in this town."

"Oh, sweetheart, this is Snowflake Falls," she said with a grin. "We make it our business to know such things."

"I...I don't...No one has ever...I mean this is all just...how could anyone be so..."

"I know...I know," Velma said as she reached out her hand and began to pat Cecily's knee. "It's just what we do here. We take care of our own."

"But I don't live here," Cecily reminded her.

"Yes, but if you are related to someone in this town, you are officially considered 'one of us.'"

Cecily needed time to be able to process what was happening. She was completely overwhelmed and had no idea what she was supposed to do or say. Finally, she asked, "Who do I thank for all this?"

"Don't you worry about that. I can clearly see the appreciation on that pretty face of yours. I'll let everyone know that you were grateful. Now...let's see about getting you into your room." She abruptly stood up and grabbed hold of Cecily's hand to help pull her out of the chair. "Follow me!"

Cecily felt as if she were being dragged back into the lobby. It was hard to keep up with this energetic woman. She was winded as she returned to the other side of the counter, so much so, that she had to take a few moments just to catch her breath.

"Just fill this out." Velma pushed a form in front of her. "I know you only reserved a room for one day, but we'll leave you be until your dear husband is out of the hospital."

"Thank you. I appreciate that," she said as she took one of the pens from the small pot sitting on the counter. It had a plastic daisy attached to it. Some of the green floral tape that was wrapped around the pen was beginning to fray, leaving a sticky residue on her fingers. After filling out the form, she looked around for something to wipe her fingers on, but had to resort to wiping them on her expensive wool pants.

Velma pulled a key off a hook attached to the wall. There was a triangular plastic key ring attached to it that read *Room 4*. "I've put you in our most recently remodeled room. It used to be our bridal suite, but I turned it into the lilac room. I even found some lilac scented spray. I think the room smells just heavenly. It will remind you of a warm spring day even though it's snowing like crazy outside." She grinned as she handed the key to Cecily. "I hope you'll feel at home here at the Snowflake Falls Motel. We have a continental breakfast every morning starting at six-thirty.

That's when you'll want to get here so that you can get one of
Ginger Markle's cinnamon rolls fresh from the oven!"

The thought of more food caused Cecily to frown. "All
this food, I don't know where to put it."

"I'll store it for you. Don't you worry! If I run out of space
here, I'll bring it over to our church."

"Thank you. I'm wondering if I might have some
assistance with my bags."

"Sure thing!" She turned her head and looked back into
the area where her apartment was. "Earl!" She yelled. "Come out
here and help one of our guests with her luggage.

A tall, balding man wearing a flannel shirt and denim
overalls appeared in no time. "Well, hello there! Welcome to
Snowflake Falls!"

He shook Cecily's hand so hard she feared he might yank
her shoulder out socket. He then held open the door, letting a gust
of cold air fill the lobby.

"Be quick about it, Earl! The poor thing will catch her
death of cold." Velma grabbed something from under the counter
and rushed around the counter. She carried a multi-colored afghan
in her hands and wrapped the thick blanket around Cecily's
shoulders. "There now, I just finished knitting this one. You put
that on the end of your bed tonight. It'll keep your toes nice and
toasty!"

Cecily was both appalled and yet in awe of the overly
friendly couple. "Is everyone here in town as friendly as you two
are?"

"I'd say so," Earl said as he patted her back while
ushering outside.

"Why?" She asked sincerely. She had never met people
like this before.

"Why? Hmm…" He scratched the top of his head. "No
one has ever asked me that before. To be honest, I don't rightly
know, but it could be that we have all been so blessed by the good

Lord that our cups are just overflowing with gratitude. We can't help but smile because of it."

Cecily looked at him curiously to see if he was teasing her. It didn't take her long at all to realize that these people didn't have much at all in the way of material things. Their apartment appeared to be about the size of her living room back in Chicago, and yet they both seemed genuinely happy. It didn't make sense at all to her as she opened the trunk for him. He reached down and pulled out all the luggage as well as the bags of gifts they had brought for their grandchildren.

"You were only planning to stay one day?" He asked with a smirk on his face as he threw the carry-on strap over his shoulder. He gathered up all the bags of gifts in one hand and then took the handle of the largest suitcase in the other. He'd have to come back for the others.

"Well, you just never know what to wear," she said, now feeling guilty that she had asked the elderly man to help. "Here, let me take some of those bags."

"You just go up ahead and open the door. I've got these just fine."

As soon as Cecily opened the door, a sweet, sickly aroma slammed hard against her nostrils. She immediately began to cough as she looked for the light switch. She then noticed how cold the room was. "Is there a heater in this room?"

"Just a floor heater. We still have to put new heat in. The old ones all gave up the ghost last winter." He put the bags down, then hurried outside to retrieve the others.

She looked around the room and found a small electric heater plugged into the wall. She walked over and turned it on high. Just then Earl was coming back in with a second load of luggage. "You can place those anywhere." She dug down into her purse and pulled out her wallet. She took out a twenty dollar bill and handed it to him. "Thank you again for your help."

"Put that away! I'm not taking your money. You'll need that to pay the hospital bill!"

"We have very good insurance. Please, take it. I appreciate your help."

"I'm not taking your money." He turned to leave the room saying, "If you need anything else, just holler."

"Holler? Um…" Again, she wasn't sure if he was being serious or not.

"Dial zero." He laughed by her apparent confusion. "Though if you did holler real loud, I suspect we'd hear ya." He gave her a teasing wink, then shut the door behind him as he left.

Cecily placed her hands on her hips as she looked around the very purple room. Velma was right in calling this the lilac room. From the bedding, to the wallpaper, and the pictures on the wall…lilac flowers were every where. She wondered what Winslow would think of the room. "He would say, Cecily, think of it as an adventure, my dear," she mimicked his deep voice. She chuckled softly as she sat down on the bed. She then began to cry as the day's events finally caught up to her. The reality of her husband of over 40 years having a heart attack was more than she could handle.

She was just blowing her nose when the phone rang. She sniffed several times, then answered. "Hello?"

"Hi there! This is Velma. I just wanted you to know you have a couple of beautiful flower arrangements here in the office. One, I believe, is a Christmas Cactus. It's in full bloom and simply spectacular!"

"Who are they from?" She asked, still confused that anyone knew she was in town.

"There's a card, but I didn't open it. That would be snooping…but I suspect that at least one of these arrangements came from the Methodist church ladies. They wouldn't want to be out done by the Lutheran Ladies' League. I'm sure they heard about all the food and thought they'd better do something, too."

"Um…can I leave them there in the office? I was just about to dress for bed."

"Of course! But...oh...I see your sweet daughter-in-law heading this way. She must be here to see you. I'll send the flowers down with her."

"Carol's here?"

"Yes...hold on, she just entered the lobby.

Cecily could hear mumbling in the background before Velma returned to the phone and asked, "Mrs. Brunswick? Are you still there?"

"Yes, I'm here."

"Carol is heading down there right now."

"Could you stop her and let her know…" She stopped when she heard the knock on her door. "Never mind. She's here now."

Cecily hung up the phone, then took a deep breath. She wiped at her eyes with a tissue, then opened the door. As soon as she saw her daughter-in-law standing at the door, she immediately began to cry again.

Chapter Twenty-three

"Oh, Cecily! I'm so sorry. You must be worried sick about Winslow," Carol said as she entered the room. She placed the flowers on the desk, then seeing tears in Cecily's eyes, she reached for a tissue box and pulled out a few sheets and handed them to her.

"Don't mind these tears," Cecily said as she sniffed. "It's just been a very long day for me. I'm just exhausted." She took the tissue from Carol and began to dab at her eyes.

"I understand. I'm sorry to stop by so late, but I wanted to know how Winslow was doing?"

"He is doing very well. He's been well cared for at the hospital. It's quite small for a hospital, but the doctors and staff have treated us so kindly, and the people here have been…" She shook her head, still so amazed by the outpouring of love and support.

"They are good people here, and they truly care about others."

"Yes, I am learning that. It's not as terrible of a place as I've always made it out to be." Cecily motioned for her to have a seat on the wobbly desk chair while she sat on the edge of the bed. "It's a very…interesting room, wouldn't you say?"

"Yes," Carol said, trying not to laugh. "Velma and Earl have owned this place since as far back as I can remember." She looked around the room. "I can see that nothing much has changed since it first opened."

"Really? She told me this room had recently been remodeled."

Carol shook her head and laughed. "That just means new bedding and new plastic flowers were added."

"Oh, I see...well…" She nervously ran her hands down the creases of her slacks as she looked closely at Carol, noticing how healthy and happy she looked. "You look really good, Carol," she said earnestly. "I feel like I haven't seen you in such a long time."

"It has been a little while, and thank you, but after my recent ordeal, I imagine I look pretty rotten. I'm assuming you heard about it."

"Yes...I..." She hesitated. "We came to see the children, and I wanted...well, you know what I wanted, but..."

"Yes, I know." She reached down inside her purse and pulled out a small box. She held it out to Cecily. "I want you to have it."

Cecily took the box and opened it, revealing her mother's wedding ring. She took a deep breath in, then slowly blew it out. "Why don't you want it anymore?"

"Because I will no longer be wearing it, and I understand how important it is to you."

Carol shook her head. "I thought it was important to me until today. Nearly losing Winslow has made me realize what's most important."

"But the ring…"

"It stays in the family, that's all I ask." Cecily closed the lid and handed the box back to Carol.

"I promise," Carol said as she placed the box back inside her purse.

"Thank you...and please forgive me for making such a big deal about it. I've been thinking quite a lot today about all sorts of things. Winslow means the world to me. I should have told him that more. I should have told Paul and the children…and you. I should have told you…" Her head lowered as she began to cry again.

Carol reached out and placed her hand over Cecily's. She had never seen her mother-in-law like this before, so she wasn't sure what to say or do.

"Carol…" Cecily said with her head still lowered. "I did something...I was just...I don't know...jealous I guess. I never wanted Paul to love you."

"I know you didn't."

"He did, you know?"

"He did what?"

"He loved you."

Carol began to shake her head, but Cecily held up her hand for her to stop. "He loved you very much, but I kept nagging him about marrying you. I told him fabricated stories to make you look bad. I manipulated him to believe that you were...well...I'm just so sorry. I can't undo it. He's gone now, but I still need to make it right. I need you to know the truth."

"The truth? What do you mean?"

"The truth that you were..." She sighed heavily before raising her eyes to look directly into Carol's. "The truth that you were perfect for him."

"Cecily...your son was going to leave me. I found divorce papers." She blinked her eyes, trying desperately not to cry.

"Yes, but did you notice that they weren't signed. I was the one that filled them out for him, but he wouldn't ever sign them. He talked about going to marriage counseling, but I kept telling him that counseling wouldn't work. I just kept hounding him to sign the papers. It was me who wanted him to end your marriage...not him. He never wanted that."

"Oh, Cecily. I..." Carol could no longer fight the tears. "I don't understand. He told me that he didn't love me and that he was leaving. My children heard him say that. Blake is still worrying about it...my parents said that he mentioned it to them just yesterday."

"I can assure you that he was merely speaking out of anger. Paul was always like that, even as a child. If he didn't get his way, he would say the most ugly things to us, but he always later apologized. I know he would have apologized to you...if he had had the chance."

"I don't know...he was very angry that night."

"Honestly, I think he was more stressed than angry. His finances were a mess, and his business wasn't doing well at all.

We were going to have to help bail him out yet again. He never could seem to manage his money very well."

"He never told me. I just assumed everything was okay."

"Paul was a proud man. I can assure you, Carol, that things were not okay at all. He was asking us for quite a bit of money."

Carol reached for a tissue and began to wipe at her eyes. "Thank you for telling me this. I've really been struggling with his last words to me."

"Do you know what his last words to me were?"

"I'd like to know." Carol nodded her head.

"It was just the day before he died. He had called me during his lunch break. He was telling me how Blake wanted to be a football player. He was so proud of that and was looking forward to watching him play. He also told me that he wanted to get away with you and wondered if I would watch the children for a few days."

After hearing this, Carol dropped her head into her hands and allowed the flood of emotion to wash over her. The tears seemed to bring healing to a heart that had been broken for so long.

Cecily placed her hand on Carol's shoulder while she cried. "You were a good wife to our Paul, and a good mother to his children."

It took a while before Carol was able to look up again. She reached for the tissue and wiped at her eyes. "Thank you…You don't know how much this all means to me."

"I wish I had told you sooner."

"I'm just glad that you did now. It will help me be able to move forward."

"The children need you, Carol. I know that you will always be there for them."

"I will. I hope that you'll be there for them, too."

"I would like that very much," Cecily said as she bean to dab at her eyes again.

"Speaking of the children, I hope that you will be able to stay until next week. Lizzie is in her first Christmas pageant, she's going to be an angel. She's been rehearsing like crazy."

"Oh, that sounds lovely. The doctor said that Winslow only needs a few days in the hospital. We'll then make some other arrangements as to where to stay. Is there another hotel in town by chance?"

Carol began to laugh. "Sorry, I'm afraid this is it, but my parents have plenty of room. You can stay with us."

"That would be nice. Tell your parents I come with lots of food, enough for a Christmas feast I would guess." Cecily began to laugh.

Carol couldn't believe what she was hearing and seeing with her own eyes. "I think this may be the first time I've ever heard you laugh. You look simply radiant with that smile on your face."

Cecily, who was always so prim and proper, looked into the mirror to see the smile herself. "Well, look at that! I do look rather stunning, don't I?" She chuckled softly.

"Yes, you do." Carol stood up then. "Well, I know it's late so, I better get going. I'll bring the kids by tomorrow. Maybe we can all go to the hospital together to see Winslow."

"Yes, Winslow would love that so much. He misses the children...I miss them, too."

"They have missed you both very much."

Without saying anything else, Cecily reached out her arms and pulled Carol close. It was the first time Carol had ever been embraced by her. It was a hug that brought healing as well as forgiveness.

She turned to leave, but then stopped when Cecily asked, "Before you go, could you tell me if I should be concerned about a man named Floyd?"

"Floyd Emerson?" Carol asked.

"Yes, I believe that was his name. He was the man who called to tell me that you were missing."

"Oh...I see. No, I wouldn't imagine you would have anything to worry about with him. But be warned, if he reaches out to give you a hug, be sure to take a deep breath first."

"Why is that?" Cecily's eyebrows raised.

"Because he will squeeze the air right out of you!"

"Oh, my…" Her eye's widened. "I don't know what to think about all these people here."

"Just give it some time…they have a way of growing on you."

"Like a weed?" Cecily asked jokingly.

"No…" Carol shook her head as her eyes took in all the purple in the room. "More like a lovely lilac bush."

"Plastic or real?" Cecily began to laugh again.

"Maybe a little of both." Carol joined in her laughter.

Chapter Twenty-Four

The church was packed to overflowing for the special Christmas pageant performed by the preschoolers from the St. Timothy Lutheran Preschool. The front of the church had been transformed into a lowly stable complete with a manger full of hay and a bright star that hung from the ceiling. The children, dressed as angels, sheep, shepherds, wise men, and of course, Mary and Joseph, stood around the stable with faces all aglow as they happily shared the familiar story of that first Christmas long ago.

The teacher, Harriet Carrington, and her assistant, Darlene Bigsby, had been using this same pageant for many years. Although the lines and costumes were the same, there was always a little uncertainty about how the actual performance would go. When it was all said and done, they were pleased with how well the children had done reciting their parts. However, there were a few mishaps. First the wings fell off one of the angels, causing some emotional tears. The play had to come to a complete stop so that Harriet could run up onto the stage to help put the wings back on and dry the tears away.

Then the donkey, Kyle Bradley, decided to "moo" instead of "hee-haw." Though it brought a roar of laughter from the audience, it upset Patrice Schmidt, who had the coveted role of Mary. She was so upset that Kyle wasn't making the correct sound for a donkey that she dropped the baby Jesus back into the manger, marched over to Kyle, and angrily slugged him in the arm.

Patrice was rather bossy, and even at four-years-old she demanded perfection. Because she was playing the role of Mary, she would call it "her play" which the other children didn't like one bit, especially, Kyle. He knew the mooing would upset her, that's why he did it. Since he was taught never to hit girls, he didn't respond by punching her back, instead he simply looked

Patrice in the eye and mooed even louder, causing Patrice to run off the stage wailing at the top of her lungs.

Keith covered his eyes with his hands and quietly groaned. "Oh, that boy of mine."

Carol had covered her mouth with her hand to keep from laughing. She leaned over and whispered in Keith's ear, "I wonder if he gets that from his father?"

Keith wrapped his arm around Carol's shoulders, and whispered back, "He does. I'd be worried if I were you."

She smiled as she shook her head to let him know she wasn't worried at all. When Lizzie took the spotlight, she sat up straight in her chair feeling just as nervous as Lizzie had been earlier that evening. While Carol had helped her with her costume, Lizzie complained, "I don't want to do it, Mommy. I'm not going to do a good job."

"You've practiced your lines, Lizzie. You're going to do just fine."

"But…my stomach hurts."

"It's just nerves, sweetheart. It will feel better once your part is over. Don't be afraid. You've got this...and guess what?"

"What?"

"You have the most important part in the play."

Lizzie shook her head. "No, Patrice said she does."

"Her part is important, too, but you are the one who gets to tell everyone that Jesus is born."

"I know, but…"

"You've got this, Lizzie," Carol said as she bent down to look her daughter in the eye. "I know you can do it."

The little angel's eyes were misty as she bravely nodded her head. Carol wasn't sure what else she could say to help her daughter to overcome her fears, but then she didn't have to. Kyle walked over, took Lizzie by the hand, and said, "This is going to be so much fun!" That's all that was needed for Lizzie to finally smile and stop worrying about her part.

Carol's stomach did a quick flip flop as she watched Lizzie slowly walk up to the microphone. Her eyes then filled with tears as Lizzie quietly spoke into the microphone.

"Fear not: for, behold, I bring you good tidings of great joy...um…" Lizzie frantically looked around for her teacher.

"Which shall be to all people," Harriet whispered from off stage.

"Yeah...which shall be to all people. For unto you is born this day in the city of David a Savior...a Savior...um...which is...Christ the Lord!" She shouted the last part as loud as she could, now grinning happily that she had remembered all her lines. Her joyful exuberance resulted in both grandfathers clapping and shouting "Bravo!"

Of course, both grandfathers were quickly jabbed in their sides by the grandmothers who loudly whispered for them to stop making a fuss until the end of the play.

The children sang *Away in the Manger* as their closing song. Once it was over, they received a long and hearty applause along with a standing ovation. The friends and family members then made their way to the fellowship hall for a punch and cookie reception where the children were further congratulated for their grand performance.

It was during the reception that Carol took the opportunity to introduce Winslow and Cecily to Keith. "I'd like you to meet Dr. Keith Bradley. He's my…" She stopped and looked up at him, not sure what she should call him.

"Carol and I have just started going steady," he said, giving her a quick wink.

Floyd was just a few feet away and had overheard the conversation. He bolted over to them, putting his arms around both Keith and Carol. "Did you say that you two were going steady?"

Keith laughed. "It's kind of just a joke between Carol and I, but yes, we'll be spending quite a bit of time together."

"Would you say that you two were best friends?"

Carol looked at him curiously. "I'd say we are friends, yes."

"But best friends. Do you think you might be best friends?" Floyd asked, nodding his head in an attempt to get them to agree.

Keith laughed. "We're not in grade school, Floyd."

"I know, but someone...I won't mention any names...had a special request of Santa this year."

"Ah...so I'm finally going to hear what Lizzie asked for," Carol said. "But before I do, let me introduce you to Winslow and Cecily Brunswick. I believe you spoke with them on the phone."

"Well, now," Floyd said as he slowly removed his arms from around Carol and Keith's shoulders. He then moved in the direction of Winslow and Cecily.

His height and demeanor were so overpowering it startled Cecily. She took a step back and bumped into Magnus which then sent her forward, straight into Floyd's arms. He wrapped his arms around her and pulled her up off the floor as he squeezed her tightly. "I am as happy as a dog with two tails to make your acquaintance!"

"Yes, um…" Cecily was clearly rattled by the overly affectionate hug. Once he released her, she ran a shaky hand through her hair. She then attempted to smooth down her dress that had gotten all bunched up while in his arms.

"I believe we got off on the wrong foot, but I'm hoping to fix all that with you and your husband," he said as he shook Winslow's hand. "If you're in town for a few more days, I want to have you all over for some supper."

Winslow looked at his wife to see what she thought of Floyd's invitation. He was glad to see the slight smile on her face. It was a rare occurrence for him to see her smile which in turn brought a smile to his own face. "Thank you. We will be here until after the New Year, so yes, we would love to have dinner with you."

"Yes, thank you." Cecily said. "It would be our pleasure."

"Nope, it would be all mine!" Floyd patted them both on their shoulders, sending them a few steps back at the mere force of what he thought was a gentle pat. "Sorry, sometimes I forget that I'm a rather large man." He then turned back to Carol and Keith, "Now...back to you two. Carol, your Lizzie wanted for her sweet mama to have a new best friend for Christmas. So, I'm going to need you two to hold off on this going steady stuff, and let her know that you are best friends instead. Do you think you can do that?"

Keith laughed. "Sure, I'd love to be Carol's new best friend."

Carol joined his laughter, but with fresh tears in her eyes. "I can't believe that's what she asked for."

"Oh, there's some doll she wanted, too. Nova and her ladies' tea club have already taken care of that."

"When do you plan to deliver the gifts?" Keith asked. "I want to make sure that I'm home."

"We want everyone at church on Christmas Eve, so we'll go door to door the day before. I'll be dressed as Santa, of course." He laughed.

"The children will love that."

"If you need some help, I'd be happy to offer my assistance," Winslow said.

"I have an elf costume with your name on it!" Floyd said happily as he slapped Winslow on the back. "You better be careful, though, you might have so much fun you'll want to move here so you can play Santa's elf every year!"

Winslow looked at his wife. "I do love it here...and I have three very good reasons to make the move."

Cecily took Winslow's hand in hers. "This place...and the people..." she said as he shook her head making Winslow believe she wasn't keen on the idea of moving.

"I know. It's not at all like Chicago. I'm sure it will take some time to adjust, but...

"But…they do have a way of growing on you, don't they?"

"Yes, they do," Winslow said with a smile. "Yes, they do."

***

Keith had brought Lois and his boys to Carol's house to wait for Santa to arrive with their gifts. The house was filled with the sweet smell of Christmas cookies mingled with hot apple cider. Christmas music was playing in the background, but it was mostly drowned out by the chatter and laughter that filled the home as they waited for Santa's arrival.

Keith and Carol had managed to find a quiet corner where they happily watched their children playing together as friends. "I'm so glad they all get along so well," Carol said.

"The boys were excited about coming over here this evening. It's all they talked about today."

"We're totally outnumbered by them," Carol informed him with a grin.

"Yes, but we are both blessed to have a lot of support here."

Carol nodded her head in agreement. "You know, all I could think about before I decided to move back home was that if I came home, things were just going to end up being worse than they already were. I didn't believe it was the right thing for me to do, but then it got to the point that I knew I didn't have a choice."

"Is that still how you feel?"

She shook her head as she reached over and took his hand. "No, it's not. I feel like coming home has saved my life. I never imagined what would be waiting for me here. I never imagined I would find the perfect job. It's been wonderful working with you."

"I've never been as excited to get up and go to work as I have been this past week. I've even gotten to work early just because I know you'll be there in those cute scrubs you wear."

"I also never imagined that I would meet someone like you." She stopped to shake her head, still not believing this was all real. She looked up at him lovingly, but then began to frown when she saw his face. He looked worried.

Keith nervously rubbed his hands together. "Carol…we haven't known each other for very long."

He looked so serious that Carol was now worried that he was having second thoughts about their relationship. "What is it Keith? You look so…"

"I just think you should know…" He hesitated, thinking this probably wasn't the time or place to tell her what was on his mind.

"Know what?" She asked.

"I think it's show time," Keith said as he stood to his feet after hearing the doorbell ring.

"Ho! Ho! Ho!" Floyd's boisterous voice filled the room just as soon as he entered the home carrying a large bag over his shoulder. Winslow, dressed as an elf, was right behind him, laughing as the children gathered around them in a circle.

Floyd handed the bag to Winslow then said, "Let's see now, who will be first?" He looked down at Blake. "I believe this young man wanted a football."

Winslow reached inside the bag and pulled out a football signed by Floyd's son, Micah Emerson, only he had signed it as *The Monster* which was his NFL nickname.

"Wow!" Blake shouted when he saw the signature. "Mom! The Monster signed my football! Wait until all my friends see this!"

"That's not all," Santa said. "The Monster will stop by after Christmas to give you some tips to help you become a football star one of these days."

"Wow!" He tucked the ball under his arm and went to show it to his grandparents.

"Now, let's see, if I recall Bobby here wanted a horse."

Bobby stepped forward grinning from ear to ear.

"Well, Bobby, I hate to tell you this, but Santa had some trouble with the city on that one. You see, you can't have a horse where you live."

Bobby's face dropped. "I know," he said sadly.

"Yes, but did you know that my good friend, Silas Gardner has a horse named Maggie. She doesn't get much exercise, so Mr. Gardner agreed that he would let you ride Maggie whenever you wanted. He's even willing to teach you how to ride. Would you be willing to help him out?"

"Yes!" Bobby exclaimed. "Dad, can I?"

"Absolutely, buddy." Keith shook his head in awe that somehow Floyd had figured out how to give his son what he had wished for.

"In the meantime," Winslow said, handing a book to Bobby. "We have a book all about horses for you to read."

"That's right. You read up on this for a few days so that you'll be all ready to meet Maggie and go for your first ride," Floyd said.

"Thanks!" Bobby took the book and ran to show it to his grandmother.

Floyd and Winslow handed out the rest of the toys, leaving Lizzie for last. Floyd walked up to Lizzie and handed her the doll she wanted. He then said, "This is a very a nice doll, but I know you wanted something else." He looked over at Carol and Keith and motioned for them to come over to stand next to him. "I am happy to say that your mommy has a new best friend, just like you do."

Lizzie looked at her mother and Keith. Though she knew that they were becoming close, seeing them together now and knowing she had been given exactly what she had asked for caused her to burst into tears.

"Are those happy tears?" Floyd asked, a little worried that Lizzie had changed her mind about what she had asked for.

She wrapped her arms around Santa's legs as she nodded her head, still too overcome with emotion to speak. Floyd picked her up into his arms and let her cry on his shoulder. The room became silent for just a few minutes as they watched Santa gently pat Lizzie's back, with tears of his own falling down into his thick beard. "God loves you very much, Lizzie. He knew exactly what you needed, and He also knew what your mother needed." He looked over at Carol and gave her a nod.

Keith held his arms out and said, "Lizzie, will you come to me for a second?"

She lifted her head off of Floyd's shoulder and reached out her arms. Keith pulled her into his arms then shifted her to one side. He then draped his other arm around Carol's shoulders, knowing this was the perfect time to say what he needed to say. "I would like to take this opportunity to announce to Lizzie and to everyone else here...especially Carol..." He looked down at her and smiled. His eyes became misty when he realized what he was about to say. "I think all of you should know that I am in love with my new best friend."

Carol immediately burst into tears just as Lizzie had done. She wasn't yet able to speak, so she mouthed the words, "I love you, too."

Epilogue

The bell at St. Timothy Lutheran church resounded throughout the entire community of Snowflakes Falls joyfully announcing the recent nuptials of Carol Brunswick and Keith Bradley. It had been a beautiful wedding with no expense spared, mostly paid for by Winslow and Cecily Brunswick, who had insisted it was their wedding gift to the couple. Many believed it was the loveliest wedding they had ever attended. However, there were others who were not at all impressed and thought it was unnecessarily opulent and a bit too braggadocious for the humble community that Winslow and Cecily now called home.

The father of the bride, Magnus Engle, had nervously escorted his first-born child down the aisle. He was a giant of a man at six-foot-five, and yet he cried, yet again, like a little child, when he gave his daughter away. The mother of the bride, Abbigale Engle, or Abby, as she liked to be called, also began to cry the very moment she saw her husband's futile attempt at wiping his tears away. The parents of the groom were no longer living, but Lois, as well as Winslow and Cecily, cried tears of joy that these two had found each other in the midst of their heartache.

The ring bearers, Bobby, Kyle, and Blake were dressed in suit and tie, though all three had their shirt tails hanging down below their suit coats. At first, as they walked down the aisle, they were a perfect picture of how three mischievous little boys could still manage to be well-behaved when it was called for.

It had been decided that since Kyle was the youngest, he would stand in the middle of the boys holding the pillow with the rings tied on top of it. However, halfway up the aisle, Bobby didn't like the way Kyle was holding the pillow, so he grabbed it away from him, sending the pillow and the rings flying in the air. Keith covered his eyes with his hands as he shook his head. Lois, with a scowl on her face, stood up from where she was seated and marched down the aisle where she retrieved the rings and the pillow from the floor. She then gave Kyle the pillow, without the rings, and told him to continue up the aisle. She then took the hands of Bobby and Blake and walked with them the rest of the way. She gave the rings to Rev. Pickler then turned and pointed her finger at the boys, giving all three a stern look before returning to her seat.

Lizzie and Zoe, the flower girls, looked just like little garden fairies in their matching yellow, chiffon dresses and floral crowns made of daisies that circled their heads. They had been instructed to slowly toss the daisy petals in their baskets to the floor as they walked up the aisle. They had done well during the rehearsal, however, during the wedding ceremony, just as soon as Lizzie would throw a petal to the floor, Zoe would stop and pick it up, thinking the flowers should remain in the baskets. Lizzie was having none of that. She grabbed a handful of petals from Zoe's basket and put them inside hers. This caused Zoe to stomp her foot and scream at her sister. Lizzie knew Zoe was angry, so she began to run up the aisle, but Zoe was just as quick. When she reached her older sister, she pulled on Lizzie's basket, only to have Lizzie pull back even harder. Finally, the pushing and pulling got to be too much and both fell to floor with yellow daisy petals falling all around them.

Abby stood up and rushed toward them. She scooped up Zoe, then reached down and took Lizzie's hand. Since both girls were throwing a fit, she took them to the cry room in the back of the church where she could still watch the ceremony, and the girls' screaming would at least be somewhat muffled.

The three boys continued to fight up at the front, but were quickly retrieved by Lois who joined Abby in the cry room where it was decided that the children had stayed up way too late the night before due to the rehearsal dinner.

Though the wedding ceremony continued with the sound of muffled crying and occasional screaming from the cry room, the rest of the ceremony had gone off without a hitch. As soon as

Rev. Pickler announced that Keith could kiss his bride, he placed his hands on her waist and lifted her in the air. However, this time he didn't move her out of his way. He held on tight and kissed her soundly as those in attendance cheered and clapped their hands.

With the tears and anger finally resolved, all five of the children, now brothers and sisters, surrounded their parents on the dance floor as they shared their first dance together as man and wife.

"Look at them now. Smiling like little cherubs." Keith laughed as he held his wife in his arms.

"They were so naughty, weren't they?" Carol chuckled as she rested her head on Keith's shoulder while they swayed back and forth to the music.

"You do know that we're going to have our hands full, don't you?" Keith said with a grin.

Carol sighed contently. "Yes, I assume it's going to be wonderfully exhausting."

"Have I told you how beautiful you look in that dress?"

"Yes, several times." She smiled up at him.

Keith leaned down with the intention of kissing his wife, when several hands began tugging on his pant legs. They both looked down and saw all five of their children peering up at them, wanting their attention.

"Should we take these five for a spin around the dance floor?" Keith asked his wife.

"Absolutely!" She laughed as the new family formed a circle with their hands.

"Hold on tight kids! This is going to be a crazy ride!" Keith said as he began to turn the circle to the right and then back again to the left.

The squeals of delight from the children brought several other couples out to the dance floor. The dancing and celebrating lasted for a few hours more before Keith and Carol said their goodbyes to their guests. They then planned to drive up to the mountains to spend their honeymoon in the cabin where they believed they had first fallen love.

The newly wedded couple snuggled by the fireplace, drinking champagne. Keith looked around the rustic cabin thinking that maybe they should have gone some place a little nicer. Though his friend had gone to the cabin earlier in the day to air it out and sweep away the cobwebs, the fact remained that there wasn't any running water, electricity, or bathroom, and the couch was old and lumpy.

"Are you okay spending a few nights up here?" Keith asked as he looked down at her.

"Yes, I think it's perfect," she said as she snuggled closer to his side.

"Maybe in a few months we can go someplace nicer when we can get away for a little longer than just a few days."

"We both agreed to come here for our honeymoon. Why are you worried about it?" Carol asked. "Are you not happy we came here?"

"I'm happy to be anywhere as long as you're with me. It's just I don't want you to have any regrets later."

"Oh, Keith, I don't have any regrets," she said as she leaned her head on his shoulder. They sat together quietly for a few more moments when she added, "Well, maybe I do have just one regret."

Keith, sat up straight and turned toward her with a worried look on his face. "What is it? The boys? Lois will help out with them. I know the house is small, but we'll look for a bigger one…"

Carol laughed as she placed her hand over his mouth to prevent him from saying anything more. "Keith, the only regret I have is that I didn't come home sooner."

The End

9 798362 603199